THE
UNYIELDING

GARY J. SHIPLEY

Eraserhead Press
Portland, Oregon

ERASERHEAD PRESS
P.O. BOX 10065
PORTLAND, OR 97296

WWW.ERASERHEADPRESS.COM

ISBN: 978-1-62105-241-8

I adhere to this point and a profound love of what I find there burns me, until I refuse to be alive for any reason other than for what is there, for this point which, being both the life and death of the loved one, has the blast of a cataract.

~ Georges Bataille

The sooner humanity dares to harmonize itself with its biological predicament, the better.

~ Peter Wessel Zapffe

When I tried to move her I couldn't. It was like she was glued to the floor, or impaled on something, or some things, multiple impalements, because no part of her would move. And I worked on these premises for longer than felt right. I pulled at her feet, both bare and more discoloured than usual, black in places, purplish in others, dirtied from the floor. I tried each arm, pulling hard enough to risk them popping their sockets. But still there was no movement. She stayed there, secured to the spot.

I remember I was irritated at having to open the door. I knocked and she got up from in front of the TV and let me in. It was how it went. When I saw her splayed face down on the floor in the narrow hallway, I closed the door behind me without noticing my keys still hanging from the lock. It was days before I realized they were missing.

I thought I saw her head move. I knelt on the floor and pulled the hair from her face. I noticed her eye and a streak of dried blood that ran from between her nostrils across her mouth to her chin.

I leaned in closer to smell her hair. It smelled of shampoo as if recently washed. But there was another odour, unfamiliar, not from the hair but elsewhere on the body. I put my nose to her arm and without any warning found myself recoiling so violently I cracked the back of my head on the wall. There was no pain: all there was was the smell of her body that had no place coming from anywhere.

I tried to stand but couldn't. My legs knew better than to try. I sat against the wall and tried to regulate my breathing. Distrusting what might come in, I placed a hand over my nose and mouth.

I took my phone out of my pocket and just looked at it. I read the time over and over until it changed (18:18 to 18:19). I read the second number. I swiped the screen and positioned my finger over the green box with the white receiver. I stayed like that, like something would happen without my having to do it.

They'd insist on speaking to the other tenants, my immediate neighbours. They'd say how they'd heard her through the walls. Heard me too. Seen her limp sometimes to the shops. Noticed how introverted she'd become since they'd started asking questions, offering help, sympathizing.

On the back wall of the main room, at the end of the narrow hallway, I saw a rectangle of light flash and flicker at regular intervals. I heard sounds of war from another country. I heard myself throw up over my socks and my shoes.

It felt dispassionate, but I fetched scissors from the kitchen and began cutting her clothes off. I cut up the legs of her jeans right up to the waistband and folded them away from her onto the floor. Her thighs were coated in a cold sweat, which had tiny pliant lumps in it like wallpaper paste.

When I cut through her knickers they were clean and I doubted then that she was dead. I started to talk in her ear. Her right ear, because it was slightly elevated and her hair had fallen around it like a curtain. Almost an enticement, suggesting she might be there listening. Can you believe I asked her if she was alive? I asked her more than once. I think I said at one point that I wasn't sure if I was alive, said it as if I believed there were those who possessed such a certainty.

I heard the TV, and it seemed as if the volume had suddenly increased. I imagined the person responsible for my wife's death sitting on the sofa with the remote in their hand. But it didn't stick and I somehow knew we were alone without checking.

I cut up the path of her spine. She was wearing a tight black sweater. I caught the bra strap too. I cut up each arm, peeling the flayed fabric away from her as I went.

I stood over her, waiting on an impulse. She looked as if she'd been skinned: a breed of animal born fully clothed, a kind of mucous membrane underneath, glistening and oily to keep one dermis from fusing to the other.

I went to try to move her again. She felt amphibious, a cold, translucent slime coating all but her extremities. But it seemed just seconds later less like a layer on the skin and more like the skin itself, the skin's surface undergoing some sort of degeneration.

I walked around her body in the narrow hallway, stepping over her limbs, her hands and feet only an inch or so from the wall.

My phone rang and I answered it without speaking. It was my wife's sister. She was excited: *Where's Petra? Where's Petra?* I said she wasn't in. She should ring back. *So much to tell her. The party. Other things. Less than a month now.* We would be there wouldn't we? I said that we would. The conversation lost momentum and ended. I held the phone in my hand, looking at it as if an answer might appear there, looking for somewhere else to go but where I was. The lock screen disappeared and then reappeared and nothing happened in between.

Even with her clothes cut away no amount of shoving or lifting made a difference. She stayed there in the narrow hallway and all I could do was sit and watch and wait for her to come back.

When, two maybe three weeks later, the knife went in for the first time, it released a jet of blood that hit the ceiling. It fell down on top of us and kept coming. The flow eventually eased but didn't stop. Her foot was blocking the plug hole and the bath was filling up. It was around her stomach in a ring until I pushed her foot to one side to let it drain away. But the level didn't drop. Its progress up the side of the bath had slowed but showed no signs of reversing or even stopping.

I picked up the knife, which I seemed to have dropped without noticing, and cut into her other thigh. It opened like a thick rubber sack, and so much blood exited the wound at once that it created a series of waves which repeatedly splashed over the edge of the bath and onto the tiled floor.

I watched the blood rise and consume the overflow, watched it reach the bath's rim and slide over the edge like a swathe of thick, expensive fabric.

I waited for the blood to stop, but if anything the stream intensified. There was more and more of it until I had to stitch up the incisions with a needle and thread. My hands out of sight in the blood, feeling for the wounds, pinching them together and sewing clumsily till at last the flow abated. The day after, at work, I sat at my desk and thought about quantities of blood. I entered numbers and letters into boxes on the screen, but there was nothing more to what I was doing than my wife's white knees protruding from the lacquered flatness of her blood.

I looked at my hands. My nails were encircled in a thin crust of dried blood, as if I'd been wearing nail varnish and not removed it properly: my wife's toenails before she'd stopped moving.

The blood worked its way toward the door. Shifting like some insanely flexible invertebrate. When it reached the skirting it didn't stop. I watched it scale the wall behind me as I struggled to get to my feet.

It was 18:18, the day after I'd found her, and I heard knocking. It was a woman with two children, one either side, at my front door. The woman was a friend of my wife's. The children were ours. I recognized them, but still their existence was a shock. I'd forgotten them so completely that it didn't seem possible.

They both stood on the landing looking at my face, looking like I'd borrowed it from someone else and applied it in a hurry. The woman wanted to know if everything was okay. I said it was, and she said she was in a rush, her own children in the car on their own, and she left.

I'd placed a sheet over my wife. I told the children to step over it. I was thinking of something to say when they asked what it was, but they didn't ask. They went directly into the main room and sat on the sofa. I heard the TV changing channels.

When I joined them there they were looking into their tablets.

They didn't look up. I sat at the table and woke my laptop.

I Googled too much blood.

I Googled how much blood in the human body.

I Googled immovable objects.

I Googled is it possible to forget your children.

I went back to my wife's body. I lifted the sheet from her head. Something was different. It was the eye, which was open now but had been shut. Or had I made a mistake? I couldn't remember clearly enough. I allowed that I could be wrong, and what sliver of composure remained, remained.

The children started to fight over the remote and I shouted for them to stop. The moment reeked of a former normalcy that I didn't properly understand, and yet I relaxed for a moment, forgot the body of my wife—forgot it even as I sat beside it, speculating on the arrangement of its eyes.

Four weeks and three days later she appeared on the ceiling in the main room. Her feet and hands and backside were flat to the plaster. She was positioned directly above the dining room table.

I stood on the table and attempted to pull her down. Nothing happened. I'd given up on its having any effect before I'd even touched her, but there was this need to perform. This was in many ways in keeping with my life before her death. With every life I saw going on around me. Or any life I could imagine.

Mostly she was in the narrow hallway where I'd found her.

I added extra sheets and disguised the shape using cushions and items of clothing from her wardrobe.

I just wanted to watch a film and forget about what any of what was going on might mean. I'd been so used to the world not meaning anything outside of its existence, and our existence in it, that thinking beyond that fatigued me.

It was late when I'd finished tending to her and both my children were sitting in my boy's room on his bed, their faces bathed in the light of the tablets on their laps. I looked at the wires hanging from their ears. If I let them alone they'd still be sitting there the next morning. I stood in the doorway watching, waiting for some sign of recognition. They didn't look up from the screens.

I Googled immovable dead bodies, and on the second page I found a link to a forum called The Unyielding. Alongside the link there were a few lines of text which read: *It's been a year since my teenage son died, and as is the case with many of you here, he cannot be moved. For the most part he sits in the corner of my kitchen, his head tilted upward, his knees drawn up into his body. I use a box to* . . . I clicked on the link and bookmarked it without reading any more.

I sat sweating my indecision by the body of my wife. I went back to the screen.

A woman from Texas, who may or may not be from Texas or even a woman, and almost certainly wasn't called Amy, had posted a month earlier about what she called Intermittent Deterritorialization. Others used different terminology: Sporadic Shifting, Spatio-Temporal Anomalies, Random Relocations. The latter term was far from satisfactory, given that the locations were not, she argued, random at all.

My boy was eleven and my girl eight. I took them to school that first Monday, her to a primary a few streets away from the flat, and him to a secondary about ten miles out. I was late for work, and mid-morning got an email request to report to my team leader. I told him my wife had gone missing and there was no one else to take care of the children. I said I'd need to leave early to collect them from school, and if she didn't return soon I'd need to take time off. He looked at me, registering what I'd said, for about half a minute, his face expressionless. And suddenly there was a smile. I'd not seen it before and I didn't trust it. He'd talk to human resources, he said. It would be okay.

I bought the longest crowbar I could find. I heard the flooring crack underneath her. Cautious of the bleeding, I'd packed the body side with short lengths of board. The only movement I felt was of metal crushing wood.

When she turned up in the bath, I took it as a sign that she had access to my thoughts, that she knew of the plans I'd considered regarding her possible disposal. It felt like the body was goading me to do it.

The woman next door to the right, with the small incontinent dog and the unfortunate middle-aged son, took to acknowledging me on the landing. She was amiable, excessively so, given that my wife had told me what she'd said in the past, how men like me disgusted her, how I should be put down, and now none of that.

The childless couple in their forties, next door to the left, stopped looking away when they saw me. The man would nod and the woman would raise her hand in a half-realized wave. Before long there were hellos and how are yous and smiles.

The unfortunate son has taken to squealing when he sees me. He used to growl, but now he squeals and wrings his hands, barely able to contain himself.

My children talk to each other when they think I'm not listening. I'm almost never able to hear what it is they're saying, and when I enter whatever room they're in they invariably stop. When I address them they reply. It doesn't amount to conversation. We have exchanges that concern food, money and things they want. Anything more is a strain for them and for me. Anything more would mean more than it has to mean.

My boy was out at a friend's. My daughter was in her room on the tablet with her earbuds in. I was in the narrow hallway tending to my wife's camouflage, which had been disturbed by the children's passing feet. I heard my daughter scream. A short burst. An aberration of the now usual silence we'd made. I found her staring into her tablet, grinning. I put my hand in front of her face and she looked up. *What? You screamed. I thought I saw mum. Where? There. She pointed to the foot of her bed. You couldn't have done; it wasn't her. I know*, she said, returning to her screen.

I found the number for my wife's friend, the woman with the boy and the girl roughly the same age as mine, on my wife's phone. I was glad to recognize the name. I called to ask if she'd be willing to have them the night of my sister-in-law's party. She tells me she hasn't heard from Petra in weeks. I say she's not been well. She responds as if she already knew. We don't mention her again. She agrees to take the children, and I only wonder at that point why I am still bothering to go.

A man from the ground floor I'd barely seen the whole time I'd lived there approached me as I headed out of the building on the twelfth morning. He made small talk like a prelude to something else, a nervous diversion. As we talked we waited. We both felt the words were building up to something. I'd presumed at first it would be him that'd get there, but it soon became clear that he, in turn, was waiting for me.

On the night of the party, my son answered the door to his friend's mother before I could get there. She had her children with her. The three of them stood in the doorway, the door wide open. As I approached, their eyes dropped to the shape on the floor in front of them. My son looked up at me as if to ask if he could go. I felt my daughter squeezing round the side of me to get through the hallway and out to her friend. The children looked up from the protuberance in the floor and so did the mother. Them at my children and her at me. Not wanting her to accept, I asked them in. *We should get off*, she said, and inside a minute they were gone.

An email came through to my phone as I was driving to the party: there'd been a new post at The Unyielding. Glancing away from the road to check, I saw it was entitled: The Dead Are Immoveable Because They're Not Dead. I laughed, but it was shrill like someone else's laugh. It sounded dishonest and it was: I'd been talking to her in the middle of the night in a way that people did not talk to corpses.

I'd scrubbed my legs and hands every day since the failed dismemberment in the bath, but the blood refused to budge. It shifted from place to place but was not depleted one bit. Sometimes I felt the bloodied areas constrict the skin and muscle underneath. If ever I forgot for a minute, the blood would remind me this way that it could not be forgotten.

I drove the car even though I wasn't there. I was seeing lights, the road, other cars in front and behind, people in coats walking in every direction, but I hadn't moved any more than my wife had. I was still in the narrow hallway with my wife's slime-cured body draped in sheets and padded with cushions and screwed-up clothes.

It was harder to believe in myself when I was driving, harder than usual. My movements were too automatic, too reliant on what went on outside me. If I crashed I thought this might change. I hypothesized that the fear and pain would wake me up. I'd noticed my awareness had become dulled years earlier, long before any of this, but now there was a thicker layer in place and I was more anesthetized to it than ever. Sleep was no more a nothing than being awake. And no one from the forum seemed to have a way out.

The aloneness I felt in the car was imagined: the blood was there pinching at me. I did not believe in the world and only kept going as if I did because I'd come to accept that there was nothing else. Only there were those at The Unyielding that thought otherwise, who believed what had happened to these familial bodies had greater significance than any of us could yet comprehend.

Petra's sister met me at the door. Someone else, someone I didn't recognize, a man with short ragged hair and lazy eyes, had answered the door, but he was ushered back into a room containing other invitees so that she could greet me herself. *Well?* I started to ramble about how she'd been sick the night before, all over the bed, about a doctor's visit earlier in the day, how much she'd wanted to be well enough to come. She laughed. She laughed to the point where spit came out.

I'd read only the tagline of TexasAmy's post at this point. The laughter meant nothing to me. It was just a woman laughing at her sister's being sick.

She pulled me in through the door and closed it behind us with a deliberateness that I didn't understand, like it was part of some joke. Having led me into a room half-filled with people talking and drinking she let go of my hand and stood back, waiting, like she expected me to do something. I looked back at her, at the people there, and feeling conspicuous in the middle of the room went and stood against a wall.

Standing against the wall made me want the fake aloneness of the car. The sister's husband brought me a drink. His face too seemed part of some plot. I'd drunk half of it before even noticing the taste: wine, unpleasant, resemblant of blood.

She was standing by the fireplace. It was hard to tell which of them looked the more convincingly marmoreal. A couple, forties, overweight, were talking to her. I couldn't see her mouth move, but the couple didn't seem to notice or didn't seem to care. I knew that it didn't move, that it hadn't moved in a month. I knew that while movement was implied by her presence there, it was not any kind of movement that they would recognize.

The sister and the husband were looking at me. I smiled because they were smiling. I'd been doing it that way for years, since I was a child. I sensed though that the smile wasn't enough, so I went and stood beside my wife. When I got close enough to see, I saw her face was coated in the same translucent jelly I'd found on the surface of her body. It suggested to me the kind of gloopy sweat you might find on the terminally feverish.

Her facial features had suffered from being pressed into the floor for a month. Her nose was bent over to one side and there was more flesh on the right side than the left. The most unnerving difference though was her mouth, held in a permanent grin, smeared across half her face at a diagonal. It looked like the whole thing (lips, tongue, teeth) was about to fall out of her head. I hadn't seen her face since finding her immovable, and even though she looked less like herself there propped against her sister's fireplace than in my narrow hallway, I felt the panic and mental disequilibrium was tinged, for brief periods, with something not unlike joy.

I got the impression that none of us in that house were human, or if we were, being human was not what we took it to be.

For the next three or so hours people approached us to make conversation. She did not talk once and it didn't seem to matter. And while the only replies came from me, it was primarily to her that they addressed their polite inquiries and their answers to anything I had asked. We were a couple as alike and as unlike as any other couple there. Our uniqueness was the usual kind.

The body's draw on me was relentless, but when I sat beside it, it seemed to need me less. Although, the moment I got up to leave, or I managed to think of something other than the xenocrafted rock of my wife splayed in our narrow hallway, I could still feel her insinuated in everything I did or thought of doing.

I built a five-sided box to place on top of her. Aside from the frame, I constructed it out of the same boards that had been used in the rest of the hallway. When the children saw it they commented on how the lump had gone. They walked over it as if it wasn't there. When I told them to be careful they didn't trip, they looked confused.

I read on The Unyielding how these bodies, when displaced, did not necessarily behave in the same way as they would in their routine location. I remembered the bathroom slowly filling with blood. The stains on my hands and feet that moved without my ever being able to remove them. I got up from the sofa in the main room and having picked up scissors, a bowl, and some superglue from the kitchen, went and sat beside her. I uncovered her hand, placed it in the bowl and attempted to cut off the tip of her smallest finger. The scissors stopped at the bone, but I'd eased off by that point anyway, as blood was spraying up the wall and into my eyes and mouth. I was panicking, trying to get it out, trying to stem the flow with some sheeting. I cleared my eyes enough to see and wiped at the wound in an effort to clear it for the glue. It had filled four bowls before I was able to apply it. I posted on The Unyielding, detailing what had happened, how excessive bleeding was seemingly a constant with immovable bodies.

In the mirror, my eyes had turned red.

Nobody on The Unyielding had referenced the smell of these bodies at close quarters. Despite the intense repugnance and peculiarity of the smell, I'd repeated the experience almost daily. I felt I needed to place it. Most times it had induced vomiting. I learnt nothing, and had no more words for it than I had synonyms for inexplicable. What I managed to write only detailed my frustration. But I found that others knew of the same and had nothing more to say than me. A name was given to it: we called it The Obscure Perfume.

My children became progressively less willing to go to school. I had to cajole them more vigorously each morning, until only shouting worked. This became one of the few times they asked for their mother. Soon the shouting stopped working and I was forced to guide them through every stage of their preparations, like one would old men and women in nursing homes. But they too tired of this morning drill and we went back to shouting and to their almost calcified intransigence.

My children were ill more frequently than they'd been before. Most often it was the standard nondescript unwellness that sounded just a lot like being awake to me, but I would sometimes let them stay off regardless. Sometimes it just felt better having other people there in the flat. Other times, utterly sick of the pretence of their company, I would send them in whatever their symptoms. I had this feeling more and more, and there were times when I couldn't tell the difference between them and her.

I stood at the doorway of the main room and asked my children what they'd like to eat. I could see the wires coming from their ears, but still I knew they heard me, even if they couldn't make out the words exactly. I began talking to them the way I'd talk to her in the middle of the night, or during the day if the children were out.

When I drove them to school, my children would sit in the back of the car looking at their phones. I'd talk and yet to watch them it was as if nothing was said, and they were right.

I'd get scared. It always took me the same way, by surprise, and as if it had no reason to ever stop, as if I'd happened upon the legitimate default state of every living creature. There was never a discernible cause. And it had nothing to do with my wife's immovable body.

I knew that others were as real as me and that none of us were as real as her. I'd convince myself of basic realities sometimes thousands of times in one day.

My presence anywhere felt involuntary. If I needed to be somewhere else, I didn't know where that was.

Sometimes when I was asleep it was me that was immovable and not my wife. Sometimes I'd wake and nothing would change.

If someone had ever asked me directly what had happened, what was happening, why there was a human-sized lump in my narrow hallway . . .

If I stop to think. If I ever stop to think. She is there to stop me stopping. It's like she's scared I might realize that I made her up, but then not that, because it is more like she's scared I'll realize I made myself up, and she will have no one to sit with her, feel the slime on her back, smell her smell that can't be smelled.

The posts on The Unyielding became thematically similar for an entire week, some two-and-a-half months after, as we all discussed the likely circumstances of our own deaths and whether or not we too would become immovable like them. Statistically the chances were slight, but many of us felt we were already more than halfway there. Death for us had ceased to be a future catastrophe and became instead a process, the final stage of which would escape our attention. I often looked at my children as if they were dead. My guess was, it came even easier to them to do the same to me.

I am every thought I've had. And none of them were mine. It's still the same day I walked in to find her mimicking death in this narrow hallway.

Most contributors to The Unyielding find their immovable loved ones peerlessly and perennially strange. I still find the life that continues around them to be the strangest thing.

I look online for anything. I don't care what I see there. I watch whatever turns up. I let my cursor hover over every GIF, watch embedded video after embedded video, read articles, my non-existence consumed by entire hours of memetic dreck, twenty or more browsers open at once. Sometimes I follow links from page to page to page. I spend multiple hours at it. When I come full circle and end up at the page I set out from, I feel her body calling me from the hall.

In the mornings, when I return to her after dropping the children, when I have the rest of the day to live through and nothing to do with it but confirm her paralysis (which is now my paralysis too), I'm always undone by the utter insanity of being born.

None of the contributors to The Unyielding have ever met. In all the hundreds of posts nobody had even mentioned the possibility. The oddity of this omission stayed with me for weeks. As a way to stop thinking about it I drafted a post asking for an explanation. The draft remained unposted for a further week until, waking one night drenched in sweat and barely able to think a thought that felt like mine, I posted it. Over the next few days I watched the question sink to the bottom of the page and disappear unanswered.

The problem is not the restrictions my wife's immovable body has imposed on me, but the freedoms. I am so far short of being equal to them they become confinements that I cannot even enter to imagine an escape.

My neighbours call on me, at least one a day, to talk in the doorway. Sometimes there's a pretence for them being there, but mostly they don't bother. They look beyond me into the narrow hallway. They seem content with this proximity to the unevenness in the floor, as no one ever asks to come in, or suggests in any way that they'd like to.

I used to think something would happen to stop this.

I'd leave the children in the main room eating slices of plain white bread and forget they existed.

When I wasn't with my children I'd always think it must be possible to talk to them so they'd hear me, and that they could do the same and I would hear them. It never seemed possible though when we were around each other. All that happened was we'd speak and provide some texture and noise to how unlikely we all were.

I used to hope the world would return, that I'd get it back somehow and come to feel how missing I'd been instead of just feeling missing without any means of substantiating it.

To live a life you must first find life trustworthy. (The somnambulist cannot know what he is.)

LondonMark has done temperature tests on his immovable mother. She is a constant −0.01°C. No amount of outside interference alters this core temperature.

For those on the forum that were formerly religious, in almost all cases the immovable body has replaced God as their devotional object.

I came across a gallery on The Unyielding that I couldn't access. Others were trying too. Posts started showing up discussing its likely contents. The consensus was that it contained images of immovable bodies, possibly ours. Hadn't we all taken photos of our own? Wasn't it feasible that those images could be appropriated from our devices without our knowing?

Exactly three months and two days after, I had the consuming desire to merge with her. To join her where she was. To establish a physical amalgamation that would, all the time I remained there, give rise to a new lifeform. I would lie naked on top of her for hours during the day. I became resentful of the children for making it only ever a temporary arrangement.

Any initial disgust we had felt for our immovable ones got transferred back to us. The revulsion we had for ourselves, for what we were in light of them, only increased in severity. Given their conditions of existence, it was hard to see how this immunity had been achieved.

Total contributors at The Unyielding remained at a steady fifty-seven. Those contributors changed, or at least their names did, but the total stayed the same. There was never any mention of any of us dying. At the beginning I'd expected there to be suicides. It's strange now to think that I thought that.

Sometimes when I merged with my wife I'd feel that we were the only two things (the merging never reaching completeness) moving in the world, that for all the world's apparent flux it was, if you could see it, entirely still.

None of us witnesses to all this have humanness as our end.

If I ever got drunk I'd always end up hugging my children like they were two divided portions of her. I hugged as if I was trying to reunite her parts. I could feel them looking for some new distraction over my shoulders.

There was only ever unnatural light in that narrow hallway: a lack of nature that replaced all need for nature.

If I scream it's because the scream exists.

I'm this grotesque silhouette hiding in the glow of a screen that rarely sees itself. The glow is some surrogate for her. What's hidden there is always on display.

The latest consensus from The Unyielding is one I cannot help but subscribe to. It claims the immovable bodies are some kind of mysterious embryonic mutation. It claims one day a change will occur in them. It claims the change will reveal something that is not yet definable, but nevertheless needed by us. I want, but am unable, to reply that there is no need for anything to ever be different from what it is.

Although none of us admitted it, there was nevertheless the implication that we all knew how we were using these immovable bodies as potential routes outward from the world.

Within a fortnight I'd noticed how everything I ate tasted the same. It tasted the same as she smelled at close quarters. I had nothing more to say of the taste than the smell. I quickly became underweight for my height. A few inches over 6 foot, I weighed only 9 stone.

None of us thought of ourselves as insane, although we felt the presence of insanity everywhere and in everything, with the exception of our immovable bodies. This proximity to insanity made us so much more sane than everyone else that it was hard to exist, hard not to become immovable sequences of clarity with no place left to look.

If I ever mentioned her to my children they would look beyond me as if they saw her approaching from behind my back. I would always turn round. When I turned back, their faces had returned to their screens, each one immediately sucked back down into the glow.

All life outside this acquaintance with The Unyielding and its content seemed to us like demonology.

I'm in my room, two months and three weeks after, and I see the sun there again for the first time. I'm surprised to find it still circular. An oblong sun would have better fitted that nonhuman humanness. An oblong sun, made entirely from the blood and the unclaimed expirations of our undead, would have been a sun I could have recognized as such, in its being unrecognizable.

The children were off school for the summer. They did not leave the flat for six weeks. When it came time for them to return to school all the methods I'd employed before proved ineffectual. If I managed to dress them, they would just undress themselves at the first opportunity. If I dragged them down the narrow hallway toward the door they would scream and claw at the walls and doorways like cats. Knowing why they couldn't face leaving the flat made it hard to enforce the old rituals.

Our remoteness from each other became, in time, a kind of closeness.

There was a sudden increase in the number of contributors at The Unyielding. The number doubled in a day, before dropping back down to fifty-seven twenty-four hours later. The story was these were fake accounts, voyeurs wanting to gain access to otherwise private posts. I tried to remember how it was I'd proved myself eligible, but I couldn't. I didn't remember having given any proof of my wife's condition. I suspected then that it had been taken anyway. There was still the problem of the gallery link, which remained dead.

G.H.Americas, there at The Unyielding from the start,

taking the given locations as valid, had drawn up various maps marking the sites of all reported immovable ones. The patterns on the maps differed according to which sites were linked with which others. The map he liked best, and found most revealing, was one that gave the outline of what appeared to be an ark.

One morning, around five, I found my daughter sitting on top of my covered wife watching videos on her phone. Sitting there, her face seemed to have more life in it. At first I thought it was the particular play of light from the screen that had momentarily invigorated her features to imply a verve that wasn't actually there, but it continued for the ten or so minutes I watched her. I went back to bed without letting her know I'd seen her. When I got up a couple of hours later she was still there. I went and sat beside her on the floor. Later that day I drafted the beginnings of a post on the effects of the immovable ones on their children.

I began to notice that my daughter was eating much less since she had taken to sitting on her mother.

My son sat on his own in the main room or else on the floor at the far end of the narrow hallway. His appetite appeared to be undiminished.

I stopped answering my phone. Conversations had become increasingly awkward, as invariably the caller wanted to ask questions on the whereabouts and the health of my children and my wife. They wanted to know why the children had not been attending school, and that if I intended from now on to homeschool them why no legal provision had been made for such an arrangement.

The placement each day of my son in the narrow hallway

altered only slightly, a scarcely perceptible change that would have gone unnoticed had I not made a point of noticing it. Each day slightly closer to us, to me, to his mother, to his sister sitting cross-legged on top of her. The closer he got the less he ate. I documented these findings in a post, updating content in real time, with often less than a few minutes between amendments.

There was a seeming randomness to the little food my children ate at this time, and I knew without asking that to them, as to me, it all tasted the same.

Despite our lives having become increasingly sedentary, we found ourselves possessed of more energy. Sleep became harder to achieve. Out of nowhere, there was the compulsion to talk. We each removed one earbud and heard ourselves talking, more than we had in years, more than we ever had maybe, sharing banalities from our perpetual online browsing experiences as they happened. We talked over each other. Most of the time we were only listening to ourselves.

If we were dying we were alive about it.

If we were dying we knew how close that was to waking up.

One night when the children were asleep I managed to lift them into their beds without waking them. (I'd tried on other occasions but they'd woken up and screamed, so I'd put them straight back on and around their mother.) I went back into the narrow hallway and lifted off the wooden box. I removed the sheet and my clothes and laid on top of her. The slime seemed to welcome me, drawing my body into her with what felt like a greed. I had dressed and was about to replace the box when the children, having woken, returned to their mother. My daughter sat down cross-legged on her back, while my son took up his usual position by her head. It was as if the box had never been there. The reality of her didn't appear to hold the merest novelty for them. I carried the box into the main room and left it there.

I didn't know where we would end up, into which direction, if any, we were insinuating ourselves. The days for months were all the same, but the content on our screens was different. The content on each one of our screens was different to the other screens. We found enough variation to survive.

My son would sometimes stroke the cut mark on her hand and the ones on her leg. Intermittently, he would look up at me and hold his gaze until I looked back at him. I wanted to admit my mistake, if only to stop him looking at me. I was out of the habit of being looked at and the effect was nauseating.

I remembered that one of the guests at the party had asked her, conspiratorially, how she'd managed to do it. I'd asked this woman what she'd meant by it, and she said something about how slim she was and her having had two children. We both knew that I knew that she was lying.

The neighbours continued to revenge themselves with regular pleasantries. I endured their smiles and their meaningless chatter like I'd endured their loathing and their silence. I couldn't bring myself to believe that they existed.

Although the blood that had sprayed into my eyes had turned them red, it did not impair my vision. If anything I noticed it improving, getting underneath the things I looked at. The cheekbones in my children's faces. The bones in our hands. The veins in my forearms and stomach.

Our teeth were slowly turning yellow.

We accept that the night arrives without it making any difference. The same with days. It's all part of the inconsequential background to our breathing. I mark that this is not uncommon among contributors to The Unyielding: taking the different time zones into consideration, posts appear as frequently in the middle of the night as the middle of the day.

Within a month of the box's removal we were all merging with her in relay. What sleep we still needed was had while merging or while waiting to merge. Her slime levels seemed to increase to accommodate us.

If there was ever a knock at the door we all knew not to move or speak. The former posed no problem, but the latter was often difficult. We were sometimes forced to look away from our screens in case the temptation to share the content there was too great.

What The Unyielding had become was a place for us to detail our lives as if they were symptoms, and to ask questions all relating back to this common need for a cure. It soon became clear that amassment did not lend itself to direction.

Within this slow, unremarkable dream only one eventuality frightened me, and I couldn't work out whether my not knowing what that eventuality was accentuated the dread or helped me to contain it.

If a new contributor to The Unyielding read not only those posts that related to the particular stage they were at, but posts regarding all stages so far delineated, they would be able to see the future that awaited them. They'd believe that their circumstances, though no doubt sharing some similarities, would of course be different, and that regardless of the unbroken unanimity to be found on our forum there'd be enough room for them to individualize this shared phenomenon.

If we felt like pieces of something larger it was only because this larger thing was implied by a commonality of impulse. This was less a brotherhood than it was an addiction. At those times when I was able to distance myself from what had happened and successfully objectivize the three of us crowded around an immovable body in the narrow hallway of our flat, I was temporarily unnerved by it, as one would be by the horrific effects of a disease that you've so far avoided only by chance, a disease you do not have but are at risk of contracting. It was, then, as if the reality of what we were was still only the threat of itself.

When talking became a strain we replaced our second earbuds and sat there together in our separate noises and our separate glows.

Three charging cables, their plugs in a single six-capacity bank, attached or not at the other end depending on need, wound in loops and corrugations down the hallway to our feet.

My son was the first to put some of her slimy secretion into his mouth. My daughter and I both sat and watched him do it. The food had run out a few days earlier and while I'd hardly noticed, watching my son eat from his mother's back reminded me that maybe we had not yet got beyond this requirement to take on and digest other material objects. His reaction to its taste and texture was unremarkable.

We all woke at the same time unable to breathe. We could each see our own panic in the faces of the other two, and so in turn saw it abate as air gradually became available through our collective nostrils.

There was a new post at 06:01 on the two-hundredth-and-twenty-second day. It was made by PenTP08. It said, *Everything will return to how it was*. The thought filled me with a panic I did not understand. One week later: Comments: 0.

My searches became contaminated: there were immovables behind every fresh link, from celebrity diets to the increasingly desperate plights of self-harming molestees.

I noticed that my children could smell her up close without throwing up. I saw their heads reeling, that the experience was unnerving yet compelling, but there was no emetic effect. I asked them what they thought she smelled like. They didn't answer. My daughter tapped and stroked at the screen of her tablet, and then span it round so the screen was facing me. On it was some artist's impression of deep space, an almost uninterrupted cosmic darkness. *How is that a smell?* She shrugged. She placed the screen back in her lap and her eyes followed it.

Two long-standing contributors, JerzySt.P and LecomteNY, frequently weary at this point of the life, began posting on the subject of mass hallucination. I'd read plenty of posts questioning the reality of the world, the entire universe, but only the most nascent of contributors had ever doubted the reality of immovables. It seemed too ridiculous to be anything but a joke. But the posts kept coming, and our dismissal of them became angrier and more vitriolic. Soon after, the same two contributors began waxing on the benefits of us removing ourselves from the sites of our immovables, of putting at least two-thousand miles between us and *the unyielding things*. If the prospect of the proposed distance wasn't already too much, the use of 'things' sealed our disapprobation, and they were removed from the site.

Merging with her started to affect our sight. I'd noted how the walls and the screen of my laptop would blur into a single mass for at least an hour afterwards. I saw too how my children would bring their devices right up to their faces, their breath misting the already fuzzy images there.

Because we were eating less and less, there was a stench to our breath that was upsetting to smell. My children had taken to licking the slime off my wife's back, claiming it was the only thing they could still taste. When I tried it the consistency made me gag. But there was taste, so I persisted, and I learnt to keep it down.

I'd spend days suffocating in the animals people shared: cats, dogs, odder varieties of pet. It was immediately after one of these periods that my wife shed an organ. From the size, I'd guessed it was her liver, but a quick search revealed it as an acutely swollen kidney. It came out of her as if she'd birthed it. It grew legs and ran around our legs.

We could hear raised voices coming through the walls on both sides. Arguments that went on for hours and ended abruptly with the sound of someone being hit by someone or something. I'd read how immovables could be disruptive to those living nearby, especially during the middle phases.

I'd come across contributors talking about early phases and middle and even late-middle and early-late phases, but no one ever mentioned late-late phases. I wondered how they could know the relative position of the phases if nobody had ever arrived at the end. Or if they'd arrived, why there were no posts cataloguing what happens there. But the worst thing about this detail was its prescriptive finitude: why, when purposelessness and irrelevance of time had become our paradigm, was there any need to formulate a sequential and teleological framework?

The organ's favoured place of rest was on my lap between my computer and my stomach. I felt its warmth burrow down into my groin. Like us it seemed to somehow feed from the slime on my wife.

When a month had passed without us having left her side, I placed a webcam at the main room window looking out onto the street, and another in the doorway to our flat looking out onto the landing and the stairs. The feed was accessed by all three of us at all times. In the top right-hand corner of our screens the world around us played out like it was still there. It made us feel more like we were part of what was happening, like we had not gone someplace else to do this, but had remained and gone beyond it. This sense of being in a place within a place didn't last.

I skipped over it as if it was nothing, the moving away from her to place the webcams, but it was increasingly many and variant things while it lasted. It took days. My vocal cords would seize up and prevent me from breathing. It was like I was waking from a sleep I wasn't supposed to be waking from.

It got so that if I ever slept I woke up unable to breathe. I would stare at a fixed point on the wall and suffer it till I got some air in through my nose. Little by little I was breathing. Little by little I wasn't dying. It was always death at the beginning, always the last time it would happen, the time when no air came. It was non-historic. It was the end no one was talking about. And it smelled like the closeness of my wife.

My children took photos of their mother until all their devices were full. They would select and keep the best ones, one from every week, before deleting the rest and starting over. While the photos all looked the same, they postulated numerous changes.

People moved in the street outside. We watched them walk across our screens from the right and from the left. They were fully dressed and some appeared to be laughing. They went to and returned from somewhere else. On the landing we saw our neighbours. Sometimes there were people we did not recognize. We stopped moving when that happened and did not move again until we couldn't see them anymore. If they knocked on our door we maximized our internal video windows and watched them to the exclusion of everything else. The faces would begin to warp and blur and drip. When they left we watched the space they'd left from as a way of keeping them from coming back.

The light from the bulb in the hallway seemed to be getting brighter. At first I thought it was a temporary brightness forewarning its end, but instead the light just continued to intensify. Our eyes were constantly adjusting themselves, our pupils shrinking smaller and smaller until we doubted they were still visible.

My son would get calls on his mobile from people he didn't know, people displayed only as numbers. The contacts from his list of them did not call or message anymore. At the beginning there had been many such attempted communications to ignore, but now there were only the numbers. If any of us ever answered our phones we didn't understand what the people were saying. The language used had the intonations of English, but was incoherent. A garble. A prattle. A retching misarticulation. Still, there was an expectation to the voices, like a command was being given to which we were expected to capitulate. The same sounds got repeated. Got louder. The voice was human enough but genderless.

After a week the organ disappeared. We assumed it had returned to the inside of her body. Hours after discovering it missing my daughter saw it on the ceiling above us. It seemed to sit as if guarding: a sentinel, her sentinel. A week later it was gone and we never saw it again. My son claimed to have eaten it. We didn't believe him. He said he hadn't wanted to but that it had climbed inside his mouth and forced its way down.

The periods of our merging with her extended. It was the task of the two not merged to separate the third from her body. The disunions got increasingly difficult. My children often needed to insinuate themselves between us to successfully interrupt my prolonged mergings.

The TV was on in the main room. We saw the swell of its light on the wall. It had been on the whole time, for months at this point with no one watching it. The sound was down but not muted. This murmur of life from another room was an unacknowledged source of comfort to us. Unacknowledged that is until one day it stopped, with the flickering of its light on the wall also gone. We missed it. We felt alone. It took us weeks to regroup, so we again felt like four people together instead of one broken up into four separate pieces.

The slime over my wife took the place of both food and water. When we ate from her we drank as well. There was never less than there'd been before we started.

People began coming to our front door to die. They would collapse less than two metres from where we were sitting, only the door between us as we watched on our screens. Suddenly overcome by some asphyxiate poison that was also boiling their organs, cooking their interiors until the screams turned into the whistling of old kettles, they staggered around as if drunk until they dropped. When they stopped moving we pulled them in. We stored them in my son's room, the first room off the hallway to the right. Sometimes as many as three would turn up and die. When eventually it got so we could not keep up—my son's bedroom being full and the diversions proving painful—we left them where they fell. Others came looking to take them away before dying there themselves. More came, wearing masks, and took the dead. We did not see those ones die.

We watched crowds form in the street outside. They looked up in the direction of the camera, waiting. We watched them watching. The body of the crowd regenerated constantly. If we looked at them long enough we could see them in the wall in front of us, in the torso of my wife. We saw the mouths move. We heard high-pitched noises we associated with shouting. The mouths moved oddly. The sounds though did not come from the street but from my wife.

My daughter started scratching at her eyes. She went blind for an hour. When her sight returned she claimed to have seen things that were now gone. Her calmness induced a close approximation of panic in her brother and in me. We tried not to imagine what it was she had seen. She continued going blind until her eyes were virtually scratched out. After the scabs had healed and fallen off her sight returned to normal. There were no more episodes of blindness. She told us she missed them, because what she'd seen had been hers, and her mother was there and she was moving.

That there were dead bodies piling up at our front door, that

I had dragged them into my son's bedroom: none of this can be confirmed one way or the other. My children claim not to remember this part. And the bodies weren't there much later when the room was opened up. But then there were all those strangers' clothes.

However many times a day we merged with her the proximity was never sufficient. The closeness was more intensely felt than the closeness between us three, but still not enough, as if we had further to go with no way of getting there. We tried huddling together, just us three, to emulate what we did with her, but it would not be replicated. What closeness we had was achieved through the words we chose to verbalize, and the way we'd show the other two our screens like they were pictures of our brains.

The formation of crowds in the vicinity of an immovable had been documented before on The Unyielding, but we were the first to film one. For one whole day I streamed it on the site. The response was enthusiastic, paranoid yet somehow emancipatory. Comments ran into the hundreds, with contributors still asking for updates months later. Others took our lead and more crowds were found and subsequently streamed on the site and followed with near-delirious avidity. Those in more isolated areas tended not to find them. And although the disappointment in their posts was palpable, I considered such scant attention a blessing and wanted the same for us. The crowds, in keeping with all crowds, were nothing more than a pointless vulgarity.

Our hair took less than a day to fall out. Nine months and three days in, which as I discovered falls exactly midway in the predicted period for hair loss. I collected it up into a pile and left it there on the floor beside us. My children looked exquisite in their baldness. Like they'd been purified.

It was common for acolytes of immovables to long for the same death that had befallen their static loved ones. The desire was to become like them, to secrete one's own nutritious slime, to harness attendees in the same way. The obvious worry was that there would eventually be no more suitable candidates to watch over you, only a pile of greasy bodies left alone in a room, or on a staircase, or in a garden, or in a narrow hallway.

The smell of her up close still made me sick. To call it a smell is inaccurate. The smell of her up close was not a smell; the smell of her up close was a sense I didn't have.

A contributor had run the stats and none of the immovables, or us, their families, had any more in common than would be expected from two randomly selected humans or families. There was no one thing they or we all shared in, aside from the predicament itself. The data available to this contributor was of course limited, and so there could have been (could be) some genetic, chemical or biological link, for instance, that was common to us all but which we had no way of knowing. On the surface we had only circumstances to unify us. There was mention, however, of how our common diet could be altering our physiology so as to induce correlations that hadn't been there before.

In the early phases, our individual weights had fluctuated violently. Layers of fat would disappear overnight. One day I could see my children's ribcages sucking on their skin and the next there'd be rings of fat there and no hint of the skeleton underneath. This was our bodies becoming accustomed to our new diet. A few weeks in and the weight stayed on. We got larger and softer to the touch. None of us had ever been anywhere near the size we became. It had to do, I assumed, with our no longer needing to expel waste in the usual manner. The convenience of our not having to continue our former habits, to have to shit and piss where we sat, was not lost on me. Instead we would sweat our waste out into the world. We glistened like we'd been coated in Vaseline, a slippery unction, an excess that clung to us. When the heating failed it kept us warm. If we wanted we could scrape it from our skin and eat it.

We stopped seeing our neighbours on the landing and ascending and descending the stairs. We'd come to expect the mother to the right of us, her eyes and cheeks increasingly black, to walk out onto the landing around 12:00 and make her way down the stairs, and for her to return a couple of hours later. We'd come to expect the female of the couple to the right to limp out of her flat in the early morning, to return and leave again at hourly intervals. The husband to the left and the son to the right had made only sporadic forays onto the landing since I'd installed the webcam, so their absence was less noticeable. Noticeability though was not commensurate with impact, and we missed our sightings of the men far more acutely: what they did out there on the landing held a fascination for us. There was an inexplicability to their movements that we nevertheless tried again and again to decipher. The son, for instance, would run out onto the landing, looking behind him in what passed for terror in his newly sunken face. He would keep looking behind him into the hallway of his flat as if there was something back there in slow pursuit. Other times he would climb up onto the banister, clinging to the underside of the ascending stairs and looking at the floor as if some vicious animal we could not see had chased him there and was now waiting for him to climb down. On some occasions he would train his eyes on the staircases, thrashing out intermittently at objects or beings we couldn't see. The husband to the right did the same thing each time—not that this regularity, even had it lasted years, could have tempered its essential oddness—and we'd watched him do it all of those times in silent concentration. For me it was the one thing that had threatened to pull me from my wife's body, out onto the landing, to see without the aid of a screen the incomprehensible postures of an otherwise underweight middle-aged man with a stomach grown to the size of a large watermelon.

There were regulars in the crowd on the street. We recognized them instantly. But there were also expectant newcomers, there to see what the others had already waited weeks to see and not seen. My daughter thought we should maybe reward their persistence in some way: put something in the window, a sign, an object, ourselves even. She didn't say it out loud, but I read it in a mail to her brother. He told her not to be stupid and how the crowd had nothing to do with us, that it had formed, as all crowds form, for reasons the crowd itself did not understand. Or this at least is my translation of what he wrote.

Our teeth fell out one at a time. We piled them up with the hair, alongside it like a tiny ossuary. It was as if our bodies knew that they were no longer required, that there could be no possible going back from our current diet of the wife-mother's transparent goo, of our own similar if inferior product.

The light from the hallway was still getting brighter, and it was becoming increasingly difficult to see. It didn't seem conceivable that the light could get brighter, not perceptibly so, at least, but it did, brighter and brighter until it felt like our eyeballs would dry up and fall out of our heads, to be placed alongside our hair and our teeth, where they would crack and blacken in the intense glare.

I stopped reading posts from contributors at more progressed phases than us. I stopped, knowing I wouldn't be able to keep it up. I needed respite from the weeks to come, from those weeks' duplication. I read posts only from those at earlier phases. I read for differences, deviations from the pattern, anomalies I could get lost in like we might too be enacting one. The best I could find were prima facie excursions from the standard configuration, that turned out, with no exceptions, to be nothing more than an unnecessary flourish of language, or else a partial corruption in the content of an image. Still nobody had mentioned an end, despite all our talk of phases preempting it. Even the most established contributors refused to acknowledge its presence. We came to think of the end as a corrosive perpetuity, a process that eventually removed contributors from the site without their ever completing what could be thought of as a late-late phase. There was the indication too that accounts had been resumed, exclusions reversed, the end maybe reached and returned from, though it was never spoken of.

It wasn't often that we felt where we were. We were part of something immovable, in orbit to it, and we rarely looked outward to see what might be orbiting us. We saw the crowds of course, the neighbours, the perhaps spurious bodies in the doorway, but mostly we saw them without feeling we were there too. It was just those things without the seeing: the appearance, the registering of images, a desireless processing of colour and light. When we did happen to see and feel ourselves, there in the hallway around her, bald, toothless, swathed in fresh layers of fatty tissue, we broke, got chewed up on the gears of ourselves like any other humans. We all tried to merge with her at once. We did anything to stop ourselves disappearing. Our arms and legs and heads jerked and fidgeted like the husband to the right had done on the landing and up the stairs. Of all the things we could have found to fear we still feared that same discharging of identity, that same icky nowhere of ourselves, the lie of everything and the certainty of nothing and the conditions necessary to suffer it.

The day my son just got up and left us, walked into the main room and sat down in front of the dormant TV, was the day I chose to relinquish my self-enforced embargo on The Unyeilding's future phases. The desire for this to be documented (for the consolation of company) and the desire for it not to be documented (for the promise of deviation) were equally weighted. I found it accounted for more than once: a temporary distancing, that could last anything between a few hours and a week. He was back beside us the next day.

A series of new posts from the site's administrator alerted us to a dramatic increase in traffic. No numbers were mentioned, but there was talk of a hundredfold and counting. Memes started appearing in mainstream social media: images of rocks made to look like people surrounded by attendees, Homer Simpson prone and encircled by his family, his immoderate lethargy having been mistaken for immovability... The administrator updated the site's encryption, gave us all twenty digit passcodes to access the feed. This helped contain the spread, but still our browsing brought up a disturbing amount of content lampooning us as some kind of murderous subculture, a cult of demented agoraphobic necrophiliacs bent on slow suicide and the proliferation of the familial hermitage. Others labelled us as xenodieticians, and plastered forums and health food sites with demands that this slime be made available on the open market. Apparently there was the belief that the late-phase pudginess could be avoided by isolating the ingredient that caused extreme weight loss in the early phases of ingestion.

There was still the question of how she died, how any of them died, if this was death. At the beginning, we'd all presumed something pedestrian like heart-failure or stroke, as none showed any signs of external trauma. None of the houses or flats or bedsits betrayed evidence of having been broken into either. They were just there where we found them and did not move, unless we moved (as most did early on, at least once), in which case they followed us, preserving the same rigidity and yet somehow not being the least conspicuous. I'd always thought that if an end to this existed it would consist of knowing what or who had killed her. For all those who thought the cause of death came from inside the immovables themselves, as many imagined it to be external to them. I'd always been an externalist, and had concocted enough mutating variations on this assailant-creature to fill an average-sized supermarket with its manifestations.

The increased softness in our paunches and in the muscles in our arms and in our legs made merging easier and more pleasurable. It also made existing at a distance from her grueling and the slightest movement arduous. My naked lap resembled a clouded pool. And from the reflection in my laptop screen, my face was of a man having already succumbed to a slow and peaceful death by drowning.

Sometimes my daughter would tell us what her friends were doing. They still messaged her. She still followed them on social media. She mentioned the places they had visited, the pets and clothes and boyfriends they had accumulated and/or shed. I sensed something like envy or regret, but most of all I sensed a devastating condescension. Like they were babies, small insects playing at having souls. She said she thought the way she looked now was a more accurate reflection of what she was. She'd never fit into the clothes her friends were wearing, and of course the hair for the hairstyles was missing. They were pretty though, she thought, or, rather, cute, like puppies and rabbits were—all the time the fur was there to prevent you from ever seeing them.

Our respiration, when we thought about it, seemed not be happening. It was as if we were breathing at this time without having to breathe. The way our skin moved suggested that maybe it was doing the work our lungs had done. The regularity of it was constant: no fluctuations, a perfect equilibrium of depth. We were living without having to do it for ourselves, even more so than before.

From a flattened map of the planet we were near the centre. There were only two cases more central than us. And though it had not been confirmed whether or not our terrestrial positioning was of any significance, we felt those on the edges provided a buffer of sorts, though from what we had no idea and no real inclination to find out. If we sensed protection it did not matter to us from what that protection protected us from.

Our stomachs made noises that sounded like voices. We could hear our bodies from the inside the way we'd always been able to feel the gradual and sometimes not so gradual transit of our waste.

We noticed the appearance of tiny grub-like lumps in the ooze, noticed these lumps moving independently within it. At first we were wary of consuming them, but as it proved too difficult to disengage them from the slime-mass, and we were hungry then without cessation, we had no option but to eat them. We could feel the grub-like lumps moving about in our mouths, crawling across the insides of our cheeks and over our tongues, and once swallowed in our tracheas and our intestines, stomachs and bowels—or these areas, at least, because we were by now unsure as to the function of our organs, and whether or not these nouns still retained their reference.

What had been a harmless domesticated animal was by this point a serious threat. A cat from the adjoining property—large, tortoiseshell, skittish with rage and fear at the sight of us—appeared at the end of the hallway, having gained access from an extension built recently beneath our kitchen window, which had been left slightly ajar since the beginning. It stood in the doorway to the main room blown up to twice its size, mouth spitting and hissing like its face had been punctured. I'd expected it to bolt soon after, but it stayed where it was before making tentative steps toward us. We tried shouting but couldn't. We hadn't spoken in weeks, not much at all since our teeth came out, and now we discovered our voices impaired, reduced to little more than barely audible squeaks. My son did better at talking than my daughter or me, but still it did nothing to perturb the cat, and was anyway such an obvious source of distress, him having to hear his voice depleted in such a way, that he shut his mouth and did not reopen it. The cat came within arm's length of my leg, but despite my wanting to lash out in its direction nothing happened. My arms hung limply in my lap. My daughter, who had not urinated in over a month, wet herself. The cat, taking our inertness for weakness, strutted around and between us hissing and twitching, scratching at our thighs and feet, drawing blood, moving from one seated human to the next until it jumped up onto my back and started clawing at my face. I could feel its claws in the flesh over my shoulder blades. It bit on my ears and started tearing wildly at my chest and neck. I could hear the grubs inside me, like voices screaming, getting louder. Startled, the cat somersaulted from my shoulder and landed on my wife's back. It stayed there staring at my belly. Its paws sunk into her. Its legs. Its eyes grew too big for its head. We sat and listened to it cry as it merged away to nothing.

The extent of our own immobility had taken us by surprise. We'd had no problem manipulating our devices, and though merging took more effort than it used to, we'd never yet failed to achieve it. The fear we felt became a pleasure. A joy. The purest joy. The three of us grinned without our teeth. Our limbs dancing inside themselves, dancing without moving, our bodies alive in never having to move.

My daughter looked at pictures of the sky on her tablet. She liked the way its three-dimensionality suggested she take another look. I used to watch her try to reach into her screen, into the sky there. That the screen prevented her even getting her fingers inside was a consequence she seemed never fully resigned to.

A cat's skull has much larger eye sockets than most other mammals, and yet that cat before it disappeared into her back had eyes that its head could no longer properly contain.

What we did when the noise from outside got too much was push our earbuds so far in our ears that eventually we weren't able to get them out. Because we had no use for the acoustics of what was around us, for the noise not already captured by the webcams, the inconvenience, like the discomfort, was of no significance.

Although our neighbours no longer showed up on our screens, we could still hear them through the walls. We heard them hitting each other. We heard crying through the nights and them scratching at brickwork in the morning. The way the sound carried we guessed the flats had been emptied of objects, that the people were the only objects left, and that they were increasingly abstract and of dwindling mass.

If either of the two piles, of hair and of teeth, ever became unkempt, a hair turning up in the teeth or a tooth in the hair, one of us would always make the required adjustment, scraping the piles into order with the inexplicably hardened edges of our hands.

Since absorbing the cat, our wife-mother, for the first time since the start, could be heard making sounds. Or at least sounds came from her direction, from the middle of us. Or else it was someone in the flat below, having reached the ceiling, making sound directly beneath her. That there was noise in her body prevented us thinking of her anymore as dead. Or else death became something else. From what I could tell from The Unyielding, we'd discover a language in it, in the knocks and the scratches and in the gurgles. Things would be said there that would confirm our mistrust of death, that would take us further toward the end of the middle. But that's as much as I got. For beyond this the reports indulged in levels of vagueness the site admins would ordinarily insist be removed or reworded. It was not possible to read even the strangest eventuality there. It was so difficult to sensemake what was written that the concentration it demanded caused my body to revert to what had come to feel like a crude and obsolete way of breathing.

The excesses of pus were unfortunate. They arrived at the end of a sub-phase I forget. They came on the three of us at once. We oozed the stuff for days, from our armpits, from the folds in our stomachs, and in our thighs, and in our backs. The smell was death. The smell was death lounging in the sun for a week. My son wrote in a post that he thought it was death leaving our bodies. We were induced to stand and wash. The bathroom, when we reached it, looked like another planet. Though much darker than the hallway, because of the intense luminosity there, the surfaces still managed to emit a concentrated light, a light that forced their material composition to shift. The instability seemed to suck the bones from inside us. We collapsed to the floor and crawled about in search of water to clean ourselves, to remove the smell, to remove our deaths.

The world seemed a miniature thing in comparison to us. We were finely balanced on it.

My daughter looked at pictures of the sun. She Googled sun, clicked images, stayed there for hours. Her friends were in Greece, North Africa, Mexico. She was inside the sun they only felt and saw drowning in the sea. The light we were used to would blind a man. Just the residue of the light absorbed into the walls would melt his eyes, would sear his face off, aggregate his skull into a triturated heap.

The father and husband parts of me have amalgamated to include in their unified content the entirety of the hallway and by implication the whole human-stained universe.

Even without teeth we chewed. We chewed the air which turned thick in the late afternoons and early evenings. We chewed till our jaws ached with chewing. We felt our grubs chewing the same air fed to them through our skins.

The day our browsers went white we thought our eyes had been erased. The whole of humanity became that day of empty rectangles. When the images and the words came back we couldn't look at them the same. We didn't trust where they'd been. They didn't seem consistent with what had been there before. We knew then we were being lied to, that our looking was itself a lie. The crowd on the street outside was less convincing too. Less convinced of itself. An open-ended regress of the crowd it wanted to be. We watched it as if it was still there.

We heard the son to the right mutilating himself. We heard the blood hit the walls. The mother screaming. My daughter looked at pictures of the sun and smiled. She smiled without opening her mouth. My son listened to music while watching videos of decapitations in Saudi Arabia. He heard the sounds through the wall only in the break between songs. The son to the right had constructed a rationale to go with his disfigurements. His conviction to keep going was matched by his mother's that he should stop. I drew impressions in Photoshop of what I thought I would see if the wall were missing and I could turn my head with less pain. The couple to the left had turned happier than they knew what to do with. I drew them too. The images reminded me of cartoons you show babies to keep them quiet. The way I drew it, this much happiness looked like an illness.

A mid-term contributor, BenBMass, had tested the PH levels of the slime once a month since the start. His findings showed alkaline levels became depleted over time and so acid levels increased. He chose not to draw any conclusions from this data until he'd entered the appropriate phase.

All three of us missed weather at least once a week. We'd discovered a synchronicity to it. We poured over footage of the stuff until the merest notion of weather seemed a ridiculous embellishment. Like the world could happen outside the hallway. Like its inert glare didn't penetrate without exclusion. Like the frame of our walls didn't contain all feasible contingency.

We had all breeds of ersatz bird. Real birds would have had

their feathers burn up. The ones we imagined had the same resistance to heat as us. They could circle close to its bulb. They drank from a pool formed in the flat roof. They brought us information in the shape of worms and dried grass and wire and plastic cable ties.

How will we know when the end has begun? The question got repeated as many times as it went unanswered. At some point in the future I'd be tempted to go back and respond, saying that the end was already over. But by that time the impetus to move forward was too strong to do anything but progress ourselves and let what had happened bleed out.

The crowd did not understand our unnaturally transcended nature, that existence itself was something agreed upon in a séance to account for voices nobody felt confident enough to claim.

The light gets so bright we are able to see the shapes of figures through the walls. My daughter remembers being born and compares it to actors in films who return to the world as ghosts. My son and I do not remember being born and can find no reason to believe in ghosts. My son though does find reason to refer to his mother's genitals using the word 'cunt'. The look I give him suggests the word is not right, not appropriate for him to use, but neither one of us can interpret the look as a vehicle for meaning that we properly understand.

My daughter spends hours plaiting and unplaiting her mother's hair. I sometimes catch her looking over at our hair in a pile to my right. If there's a longing there for her own hair to return to her head there's no explicit mention of it. The teeth have started to blacken at the roots. The hair follicles maintain the original three shades they had when attached to our heads.

I am able to watch over the four of us as I would from the window of a train. The train is travelling at a speed that makes seeing stationary objects as anything more than a blur an impossibility. And yet I see the blur and see it as a constant, a blur that never passes from view, as if I were taking our stillness along with me at a speed that destroys integrity as a way of keeping the world in sight.

We'd wanted to die before we knew what death was. We thought the wife-mother was dead. We wanted to be like her. We still think of her as dead, because immovables are dead: it is the standard definition given by The Unyielding. And we were becoming like her without dying, or else we were dying like her without being dead. Every time we moved felt more like death than anything we'd ever understood as death. If she was dead, and we were following, we were taking life with us as a carrier for the death that was more than any previous human expungement.

My son recited prayers made from lines collected randomly from websites he'd browsed. I could have surmised he was lamenting the loss of all materialization barring the exception of his mother. But it was not that. It was a fledgling god building worlds from the world as he passed through it. The crowds outside were expecting to one day see such a thing: a god, a boy with no teeth and no hair, missing the skin from the palms of his hands, his neck, his inner thigh, suspended in blood and replete with slime tanked off the back of an infrangible mother.

We are dying over and over again of a vitality that cannot be contained by life.

The son to the right had seemingly completed his self-eviscerations and was instead chewing on the bicep of his mother's severed left arm. She stood watching him eat. There was a calmness to her that we'd seen in the part of the wife-mother's face we could see. She was without fear or pain or want—without humanity. The children wanted to invite her to join us, to come through the wall which was by then hardly there at all at certain times of the day. They called to her to come, but she stayed where she was, not moving, watching her son eat from her in a daze.

We were waiting, but more in the sense that something outside of us was waiting, waiting through us, so that we were the conduit of this other thing's patience, and had been set aside here as the afterthought of what this thing thought might never happen. This was an impermanent impression. There were other times when our narrow hallway exhausted all possibilities of consciousness. Everything in and around us a finality, the end of the world, anticipation lost somewhere in the reluctance of a carcass to become itself.

We do not share in the company of insects. They avoid us. We've not seen an ant in over a year. We could blame the heat from the light, but they'd stopped coming before the light arrived. Even the episodes of pus did not attract them, the smell of which I'd imagine would delight their sense of wonder in the foul and the sweet. That we were a danger, that they venerated what we were, that insects or arthropods or molluscs, not one, touched the floor or walls or ceiling of the hallway, led us to think that whatever our inertia, death was not since her in operation here. If she was dead, she was dead too completely to be colonized by the creatures that fed on it. She was dead in a way that could not be consumed, no matter how well adapted the physiology of the animal. She was dead like the sun is a source of light.

My daughter hoped that her skin would not suddenly stop breathing, because she had forgotten, she said, how to do it the old way. My son, without looking up from his screen, said (if the noise could be called that) that we wouldn't need to breathe anymore. I thought he might be right. But then air would get in when we spoke. Or it seemed like it should. You couldn't feel it. And then the speaking since our teeth had become difficult, the words hard to recognize, and the structures in which they were arranged increasingly eroded and meandering.

The discharge and the heat made clothing an affectation of continuity. Impracticable and uncomfortable. The clothes on the others—the people on our screens, the crowd, our neighbours—made them seem to us like animals. Unlikely humans. We were not convinced by what it was the clothes were supposed to be doing. And just like when you see a dog dressed in a suit, we wondered who had done this to them and why.

My children had their backs to it and didn't bother turning to see the husband to the left carving the names of the children they hadn't had into the torso of his wife. They could though hear them discussing the personalities each child would have exemplified had they existed.

If I had a strategy it was ad hoc and so not really a strategy.

If my wife had died before her time, she had also died after it, to the exclusion of time—an initiator, you might say, of the timelessness we discovered around her.

The crowd made its way into the building. We could see its many parts filing slowly up the stairs and past our door. If any of the parts conversed with any of the other parts it was too hushed to hear. They crouched down to look into our camera as if they could see us through it. Once one had done it, all other parts in the immediate vicinity felt it incumbent upon them to repeat the ritual, till one part, distracted from the others, did not crouch down to look and the habit was broken. We watched our neighbours at their peepholes looking out.

Posts went up encouraging us all to film ourselves and feed the footage into the site. The posts came from names I didn't recognize, but whose inception dates suggested veteran status. (Lapses in concentration were symptoms, I'd read, of the phases I'd just passed through; and so while this mitigated the oddness of not noticing these contributors, there was still oddness in the apparent newness of these documented symptoms.) Videos started appearing almost immediately, like we'd all been itching to be seen. I felt it too. And as the only webcams we had were in use, I decided we would take turns videoing our hallway with our phones, uploading the files as we went.

It was comical to see the ones with hair. More comical, though increasingly disturbing, my children finding it hard to view for more than a few seconds at a time, were those with teeth eating food. With the nourishment of their immovable there in front of them they chose to eat all manner of peculiar shaped items, some of them hard to the touch and raucous when chewed.

Comments on video links were permitted, but any incitements to push contributors to become acquainted with phases-to-come exceeding their natural inclination to do so were prohibited. Any such incitements could only prove detrimental to the contributors' development, and weren't, in truth, anything but a manipulative mode of ridicule.

Watching these videos I felt we had got to where we were

too quickly, that some phases had come undone before their potentialities had been properly used up. There'd been more to glean, that hadn't been gleaned, all the way back. Could this be, I thought, why those from later phases looked increasingly like babies? I made a point then of draining the phase I was in, of advising my children to do the same. I did not want us to end up like them: swollen, glistening, turgid lumps of speechless materials crawling over each other like the grubs in our stomachs.

About how just to go about draining the phase we were in though proved elusive and self-defeating.

Although the feeds were fed from as many different countries, there was scant reason to believe they came from any further afield than our own building. What differences could be discerned could only be discerned early on, in the initial run of phases, where there were the uglinesses of clothing, variant skin tones, language, and the inevitable facial discrepancies directly attributable to an as yet incipient uniformity in the musculature of the head. There were certain architectural features in the background of a young couple and their immovable toddler from Japan, and a hoisting beam on the front of a house across the canal from a middle-aged man, his sister and his gay immovable lover in Amsterdam, but these were details that could have been replicated anywhere, although their authenticity was not in question and of reducing importance as the phases accumulated.

The first time I saw other contributors merging with their immovable, what it resembled induced a vomiting that my physiology could no longer enact. I consoled myself with the thought that what we did was so differently performed that the two processes were fundamentally incommensurate. I took measures to ensure my children did not view the mergings of others, and if our own mergings were filmed they were filmed by me with the phone held askew of my field of vision.

Our conversations at this phase were carried out by screens and an initiatory gesticulation—itself requiring a not insignificant effort. We experienced no depreciation in communicative richness: through secondhand text, video clips, GIFs, memes, photographs, audio recordings, animations, emoji, and video games we were able to convey all things apposite to our condition and circumstances, not least because our condition and our circumstances were made up of these things. In this sense there was a directness that had before been lacking, when the extraneous layer of our own verbalizations had been added to our experiential reality.

There's talk in a thread from a post a year old that evaluates the likelihood of our all becoming or already having become (depending on phase position) a vessel for the slime we will eat or have eaten. The most provocative comment, from Nway57, argued that the slime functions like a parasite or a fluke, invited in by us, that has us provide homes for it while some as yet furtive gestation completes its cycle. Some accept that something like this is happening, but argue that the slime is a benign force. Others going further, claiming it is the corpus of God. Mention of God was rare, and when taken seriously was taken figuratively: taken to be evocative of the presence of an inexplicable power, rather than the anthropomorphic entities whose influence had been imagined by men in their ignorance of what forms power could take. I saw my own comment there in the thread: *Either the grubs grow or our organs shrink in order to compensate for greater influxes of slime. We cannot see how the internal mechanics of our physiology is changing. But the effect is a blitheness, and if it's a blitheness that kills us it's also a blitheness that was not possible before, and so a death that we have not yet imagined.*

I wanted for my immediate neighbours to eat what we ate. Their episodes of mania and anxiety were grounded in bad diet. At their centre they were empty. There is no solid footing, only flux. We were aspirational content tailored to their particularized insanity, and yet they could not see us, or touch us, or share in the cure of our wife-mother. What it means to be chosen is that most other people are not.

It was no longer possible for us to feel sadness. The word was almost meaningless, and had our voice boxes been able to utter it, there would only have been a sound, the anti-semantic squeal of an unknown animal in an unknowable pain. It turned out we had been so used to sadness that, for what seemed like several lifetimes (and it was all too conceivable in this phase to experience time in this way), there was nothing there to recognize. There was its absence. There was a fullness from the slime.

The birds returned to us from the window using human voices. They talked in the way we had talked, same cadences, same tones, same punctuated delivery. The birds were not real, if real is organic. They were recording devices and the voices were our old voices. For fractions of seconds it was hard to be reminded that we were once something else.

I could not describe the shapes beneath the skins of my children. I could not describe the lights there, their colours, the sounds that came from them into me as if my earbuds were nothing. And the crowd on the street became a queue. It ran from the landing outside my door onto the street outside and through the right perimeter of the video feed. The world was there but I couldn't feel it.

For the first time in months my body produced fecal matter. The substance was a grey sludge. It smelled like my wife up close, an unplaceable smell, but I felt no sickness.

There was the concern that I'd wake up to all the fear I'd not been able to acknowledge. If it came all at once, all the panic I was owed, I'd grind myself into such a pathetic powder. I knew that if I felt anything it would destroy me. I knew I'd left it too late to wake up. Or if I'd woken up, I'd left it too late to go back to sleep. I couldn't tell the difference. My life was just happening. I was just happening. It was less than a dream. There was no one there.

I saw the man from the flat downstairs, the one who'd approached me at the beginning to talk. He was part of the slow-moving procession that passed by our door. I'd see him numerous times in one day. He kept appearing again and again, filing through the building with the others and then at the end rejoining the queue and starting over. I could see him talking to the people in front and behind him, and them listening intently. He looked happier than I remembered him. As the time between each sighting of him grew, I hypothesized that the number of visitors was increasing.

I lived without even knowing what life was. I lived like an eye sees. I'd frequently forget that I was even doing it. The forgetting felt healthy and precarious.

It became difficult when the emotions I no longer had started appearing in my children. It was like watching someone else remembering who you were from the inside. I saw all my old weaknesses manifested there, in them, where they didn't seem to fit. Or maybe they were just remembering who they were, and we'd all been very much the same at the start of this. It was hard to watch them fighting to control themselves.

Fighting in bodies that weren't built for such distractions anymore. A struggle of tremors and blinking and tics, of desperate fidgets and wide consternated eyes. I did my best to console them, but I didn't understand what it meant to be alive like that anymore, to fear what had already killed you, to dread the sickness you were already in.

We attempted to start talking again. It was so hard to get the sounds right with our mouths the way they were. And yet the need at this phase was everything. We tried to reestablish the layer we'd thought superfluous. We made the noises we could and illustrated them with media on our screens. I had to tell them something, and I could see they too had something they needed to tell me. Over and over, when I'd thought I'd understood, I hadn't, and the same the other way round from what I could glean from their faces. For our faces were still there then, more liquid and cascaded than before, but still semblances of the old arrangement. Faces enough to be a certain kind of suffering at least. Faces enough to represent the entropy of a human sameness.

The worst of what I could make out from our communications, such as they were, was their desire to no longer be what they'd become, their desire to retreat from the present, to find their way back to something else.

My daughter's devices were suddenly devoted to the whereabouts and preoccupations of her friends. My son's too were devoted to his friends. Friends they hadn't seen in over a year. Or longer even, but at least that. Although the beginning always seemed so distant, it was never as far away as the present was from itself. The resumption they sought was too incredible to me. I had no faculties left for it. There wasn't comprehension left for going back. What there was was the wife-mother and the forward of that.

Videos from The Unyielding started to turn up on personal blogs and social media, hits on Google escalating into the millions in a matter of days. The site crashed: our responses to the exposure left unposted, festering, as we waited for it to come back. Papers and news channels calling us things too inaccurate and world-stained to stomach. The man from downstairs missing from our screens now for months. And still all my children looked at were the updates and messages of the friends they'd followed, looking at themselves via them. Their own followers multiplying like ants on a boiled sweet.

I watched them trying to move. Watched them failing. Even for someone whose nerves had been cauterized, their persistence was unnerving.

My time spent merging increased. The durations became dangerous. Although the exact threat it posed was unclear. The whole notion of something being hazardous had become semantically unreliable. The interruptions from my children were fewer, their use now recreational, their need now abated, gone elsewhere.

It took us into a new phase, but they finally managed to occupy their bodies enough to shift their weight onto their hands and knees. Once there they weren't able to move, not so I could notice, for hours. They made noises like the pain of the world had returned. I tried to persuade them to stop. The sounds I made were the sounds you'd expect from animals struggling not to die.

They spent days crawling to their bedrooms.

The singularity of immovables continued to be replicated and interpreted and reinterpreted and made a hoax of and verified as genuine and made a hoax of again until it turned into something else. Until we too were pulled out of shape by it. And the most excruciating turn was instigated not by the doubters or the haters or those bent on ridicule, but by the sympathizers, those who regarded us with pity and our loved ones as hideous burdens. Many of us hadn't felt anything at all for so long when we felt the disgust brought on by this interpretation of what we were and what was happening to us and through us.

The immovables themselves seemed altered by this attention. We sensed and reported a self-consciousness to their interactions when being merged with. Mergings started to feel forced, and the full immersion we'd grown used to became increasingly difficult to achieve. It was like the world was in there, in the amalgamation with us. And in sympathy with the sympathizers we sympathized with ourselves.

Theoretical evaluations of us turned up in all fields of academic enquiry, from science to literature and from philosophy and theory to fashion and nutrition. We were made lifestyle. We were made disease. We were made cure. We were made to exemplify the thought of Heraclitus through to Deleuze. We couldn't breathe, if we'd been able to, for being understood from so many angles at once. There proliferated videos of us screaming, as if screaming had become our adopted language.

I could hear my children in their rooms. Knees and feet dragging along floors. Objects falling over. A crowd returned to the street outside in addition to the queue.

The noises we made would remain in the world when we were gone.

The eyes on us were turning darker.

I tried to improvise a new mode of father. A new mode for when they came back. I thought maybe I should try moving, but even the thinking of it was too much. I could slide my hands across my keyboard, tap out words I couldn't speak, and move to merge—for somehow I was still able to move to merge, an anomaly perhaps, though certain contributors saw no contradiction there, citing remnant motivations and the body's dereliction of inertia—and that was the extent of it.

That our capacity for merging had become compromised was not altogether deleterious, for it revealed to us frustrations that in turn further revealed a shared urge to become irretrievably buried in the loved-one's body. We were being denied the promised escape from ourselves. There was a pause in the phase.

My children's devices bleeped and rang and chimed in their absence. When they returned it would be to new depths of attention.

By this time the son to the right had eaten as much of his mother as was possible without killing her. I saw him giving her shots with a hypodermic. She seemed utterly without care. He twitched and raged. He bit walls and scratched doors. His teeth snapped, fell out. The ends of his fingers became shredded and infected. The wife to the left wore her imaginary children's names with a delirious pride. The husband sat on the floor reading the names out loud, as if calling them in for tea. The hallway floor was thickened with their amassed waste.

The light from our hallway could be seen bleeding through the gaps in the doorframe onto the landing outside. The procession of strangers hurt their eyes on the escaped light rather than pass through and not see. When they looked down at the webcam they squinted. Their faces were flushed and sweated. They drank water from plastic bottles with a nervousness I'd forgotten existed.

Not one of the sanctums was breached by spectators. Something was keeping them out. No one could tell if it was reverence, fear, or powerlessness. I hypothesized a combination of the three, each one feeding into the other. When we attracted acolytes, their susceptibility to infiltration and arrest confirmed them as inexact replicas, as simple-minded murderers who'd chosen to cohabit with their spoils. That we could not be faked pleased us, but it fueled the enigma and concentrated the attention. We were not accessible via mimicry. Ours was the curse no one else could have, and they wanted it without understanding it, because they didn't understand it, because they knew, we thought, that it wasn't any kind of curse, but the consecration the world had told them couldn't exist.

When I next saw my children they were standing. They were walking. They talked to each other in a language I recognized but wasn't able to follow. The units slurred though, in comparison to the videoed specimens. They were dressed in adapted versions of their old clothes. Their new body shapes had demanded alterations be made to garments not designed to cover our variation on the human form and its materials. They looked happy the way the world showed people how to look happy. They looked like a repulsive fusion of this thing that had happened and the before of it. I felt sick looking at them. Only ever the feeling of sickness by then, never the event. I looked at my screen, hoped they wouldn't be there when I looked up again. I heard them beside me gathering up the teeth and the hair. I'm sure I wanted to stop them but nothing happened. I looked up and they weren't there.

The light dimmed just enough to notice.

I remembered how when they were born it was just what it was and nothing else. It was just seeing what no one had ever seen before, it was just that. And that in and of itself wasn't anything. The world had never been as momentous as it purported to be. It was just objects coming in and going out of view. And there were objects that made certain kinds of noise and that felt the noises others like them made. They would collect in sad clumps until they died.

Those who experienced prolonged proximity to immovables, from without the sanctum, were in all cases affected by it. We saw that it was hard for them to live. My neighbours were not isolated cases. Blood and secretions seemed to be their currency. Where there had been no occupants in the adjoining properties before the immovable in question had arrived, people were now moving in. There were accounts of experimental physicists and biologists conducting studies in some of them, of hallways and rooms filled with their equipment. There were accounts of those same scientists hacking themselves to pieces and eating bowlfuls of their own shit. Some were discovered suspended from the ceiling tearing their hair out with their hands. Some incorporated themselves into their instruments and died. That two such scientists had managed to cut off their own heads and exchange them without impeding motor function created a whole new proxy celebrity. No shortage of volunteers was ever reported. No report either of any more productive outcomes.

My children had not merged with or eaten from her since leaving the hallway for their rooms. It was hard for me to imagine what they might be eating, or how they'd endured themselves for so long.

What was not original was reconstituted. That's what attempting to undo this amounted to. The wife-mother was in the world reconstituted as wives were and mothers were and as the solid lump of both might be imagined, were it exuding the slime and transcendence of ours. The world reconstituted our no longer having to breathe. The world reconstituted the conjectured emulsification of our organs. The world reconstituted because that was what the world did.

My children were reconstituted children.

The hair and teeth they reappeared wearing: a reconstitution of their having fallen out in another world.

The next thing my children had in mind to be was one of those things outside spectating elsewhere, spectating the surface of themselves, a reconstituted surface, the newness of being seen and the seeing of that being seen.

They stood in the doorway to the main room watching the front door. Everything they thought involved stepping out onto the landing. They could not withstand the seeing of their mother there unchanged.

I saw from the webcam how the crowd was throwing them food through the open windows. I saw the delight there when it found its target.

For the first time in over a year I felt the surface of myself. A surface reconstituted, I was sure, by their seeing it. My back was a landscape they looked beyond to see the door. It tingled as if I could feel their seeing pass over it. I glared up at them, my descended face approximating anger in my imaginings of it. When I merged I felt my wife feeling my being observed by things that'd once been part of her.

When they weren't watching the door they occupied an area

as far from her as the flat afforded. They knew proximity was a draw. They knew their continued recovery was dependent on debilitations the hallway had erased and would erase again. They took their devices there. They smiled and I saw the insides of their mouths somehow reassembled. My own teeth and hair had been replaced, in two piles, on the floor beside me. The assemblages were gloomy somehow and clotted, like if someone were to try they'd refuse to come apart.

My son placed a mirror in front of me. The three of us knew about the dangers of a mirror in a sanctum. I referred back to the relevant posts. We weren't to look in them. They'd attempt to show only what the world would see if it was there. The mirror contained no propensity for love. All it could do was crave attention away from its true source.

Other mirrors are placed around us. Me and the wife-mother in the middle of ourselves.

My children imagined me clothed and walking and breathing through my mouth. They imagined a street with us on it and the three of us there like there was no fourth. How childlike my children, how fallen apart like adults.

Having to avoid the mirrors sapped what surplus energy I had left from merging and browsing. And as much as I was weakened, the grub-like lumps I surrounded were invigorated. They reconfigured the placement of my organs; or of themselves, if simulation had been achieved by this phase. Procedure called for me to remove them from the sanctum, or at least face each one flat to the floor. But then mirrors were ordinarily a hazard of much earlier phases. Their introduction this late had been reported only once. The contributor wasn't able to keep from looking. He lasted twenty-six days. When he looked he didn't even know he was doing it until he'd been doing it at the expense of all other looking, doing it for days into weeks. It scorched a hole into the front of his head where his left eye and cheek had been. A hole right through to the tissues of his brain. It was still there and was not grubs. At least this was what was written, but the photographs he included in the post did not corroborate it. There was no hole in his face, or where his face in the beginning would have been. There was only the same dropping away of features seen on anyone from this phase. What he'd thought had happened hadn't happened: this was the implicit import of what I'd read and seen. The hole in the front of his head was the reconstitution of a different kind of hole.

I drank the slime off my wife's back like there was some insatiable thirst behind it. But if the thirst was there I was not aware of it. I was only aware of what was happening between the two bodies left in the sanctum. I was watching myself then, as if through the mirrors, without looking at them, as if the mirrors were doing their work without me.

I could hear my children speaking. Their voices had the cadences of a chant, a febrile encouragement—a brainwash. The words were still so much mush.

I'd managed to avoid the mirrors for thirty-seven days when they came and removed them. I'd got so used to not looking anywhere but my laptop I didn't notice. But I felt the difference when I merged. Felt the difference in the configuration of my insides.

The husband to the left was sitting cross-legged on the floor. He'd gouged out his eyes. He felt around in the sockets like the sensation was worth his sight. He licked at the loose skin of his wife, now prone on her front with her legs spread. The light was so bright by then nothing of the wall remained.

My children turned up at the end of the hallway more infrequently, but when they did they were more consciously upright. And they had shoes fashioned from my wife's handbags.

The TV was back on in the main room. In the corner now, the farthest point, my children huddled round it looking at the screens in their laps.

I didn't distinguish the sound of the mirrors being smashed from the TV noise and the noise from the neighbours and the noise from my earbuds on minimum.

The deviation I'd looked for happened. Nobody had reported this, even as a possible consequence of something that had been reported. We were free of precedents. The late phases, if they came, would have to account for this deviation. Our mutation was a potentiality not yet choreographed by the site.

Our unlikeness might turn into something.

(The potential charm of our difference was not there when it arrived. It was not available to me till much later. All it exuded in the moment was the burgeoning horror of itself. And I was already too humanly dead for horror.)

At the hands of my children… From the outside this was something painful to process. An aerial view of my material manifestation in a hallway and her and what they'd done. My grubs felt the crush of it: they all collected where my lower intestines would have been and climbed over each other for days. What I felt was some of their number bursting from the pressure that built there.

A mosaic constructed from shards of broken mirrors was nestled into the softness of her back. Each piece embedded into the slime leaving no space even for a finger to get through. And I saw myself looking so many times at once. Me looking at myself looking at myself with no forewarning of what was seen. The sight of the dumb animal slippage of my mistake. The duped penumbral swamp of myself. I stopped looking as soon as I could. As soon as I realized that what I was seeing was my own seeing built directly into her, in place of her.

I ate from the discharge around her ribs.

My children watched from the doorway to the main room.

Their voices were missing.

I felt for a hole in the front of my head. My arms aching from being lifted so far from the keyboard. There was no new opening there, no tunneling through to my brain, to the grubs that had feasibly displaced it. I pushed at the skin in case my body had already grown a fresh layer of itself over the entry wound. Nothing. The mirror-hole, as I'd suspected, was an affectation of a different kind of damage.

The husband to the left took the hair he'd ripped from his head and stuffed it into his eye sockets.

I continued prodding at the front of my head expecting to find the affectation there. I was beginning to feel myself like a sickness.

As I pulled the shards of mirror from her back my children came and replaced them.

I sensed her trying to move.

Following days of feeling us dying (a state more accurately described as a slow, excruciating returning to life), with every shard I removed replaced, I attempted to merge with the mosaic of mirrors still intact. All down my front I felt the lacerations happen. My skin opening, my blood, or what was my blood by then, merging with our slimes. It proved a crude simulation. A partly reconstituted form. I felt my wife attempting to cry.

I stayed on her back for an indefinite period. I wanted for the pieces of mirror to come away with me when I detached myself. If this didn't happen I had nothing else, so I remained where I was for as long as anything can be said to last.

I was there on her back much like any object is on top of another object. The spatio-temporal connectivity was a goad. All those fat men filled with air. The entire emotive content of the world suckled on luxuries.

My children had become so sure on their feet that when I heard and felt repeated impacts on the floor I knew it was them jumping up and down on the spot. They were gleaning thrills from us. Our fatal injuries, to them, were like some juvenile counting game.

If I could have moved to look I would have seen that the noises were not them jumping up and down on the spot, but them trying and failing to hang themselves.

When I got back to my screen I learnt from the site that the attempted suicides were a reaction to their incarceration. I read them begging for someone to get them out. How sick they were of rubbing up against the outer surface of the world. The crowd screamed from the street in support. Their online followers deluged them with the thinnest tincture of affection:

a weak cordial of fascination and cloaked disgust. They responded to it with a similarly mawkish and disingenuous prattle.

The removal of consciousness could be ascribed to exhaustion, the exhaustion from the reconstitution around me of my body. I came to on the floor beside her. Down my front there were only cuts. No mirrors. And yet they were all but gone from her back. I saw the last ones sink beneath her skin as she ingested them.

She'd been made a toilet for the glass. Her back contaminated by reflections of my front. I waited for what it would do.

The slime took on an iridescence that hadn't been there before the ingestion of the mirrors. My cuts too glowed something close to vulva pink.

The formerly ingested cat was everywhere inside her at once.

The new placement of my organs induced headaches.

The light was again brighter than the last time I looked.

From the TV, sounds of war again. My children in front of it, silent. The sound from the street lessening. I saw the neighbor from downstairs pass by our door on the landing. The muscles looked slack in the lower half of his face. If he was pleased to have completed another pilgrimage no one could tell. The stain on the crotch of his trousers and the streaks down their legs told of the hundred or so times he'd let go in them.

My deviation, when I wrote it, was rejected as non-canonical. A disclaimer was attached that could not be removed. What had happened does not happen. It was fundamentally inconsistent with all other received accounts on the properties of mirrors placed in the vicinity of immovables. I was marked up as an invalidated user. My word was to be regarded as a distorted version of all the site's validated versions.

The behavior of my children was also considered doubtful. Such psychological regression in relative minors was unlikely, bordering on unreservedly specious.

Though ingested, the mirrors did not breakdown. I could feel them every time I merged. New cuts formed on top of the old ones. Her slime did not invite the same abandon, and its taste was impaired, its earlier taste tainted with what I imagined was the taste of me.

I would feel her shifting beneath me. As if she could feel the glass as well. As if its points were pressing into areas that were involuntarily woken by the resulting incisions. To what extent this constituted movement I did not have the conceptual apparatus to contemplate.

I experienced complete paralysis during merging at this time—the phase, late, the phase at that time not even permitted the status of a phase—so the only way separation happened was through undulations in her body shifting me gradually onto the floor, where the minimal control I had left returned. These proprioceptive glitches meant that I was able to experience tiny fluctuations in my otherwise stationary host. There was so much life inside her I was unsure what would happen if one of the shards broke the skin in the wrong place.

The eyes of my children when they passed me on the way to the door were an opaque jelly. Their sight though was seemingly unimpaired. I considered the possibility that they were seeing from someplace else in their bodies.

They spent increasing amounts of time at the door. They listened through the wood. They took turns studying the webcam feed on their tablet. They knocked and shouted in an effort to draw the passersby closer, to get them to touch the door, to talk back.

I saw a man erect a ladder up to one of our windows. Within seconds the man was arrested and the ladder removed.

Since the influx of humans the door had been braced and padlocked from the outside. The same was done to the doors to my neighbours' flats. A precautionary measure after what had occurred with those unfortunate scientists. Given both the light and the implosive concentration of the sanctum, the inverse proposition was a much more likely cause for public concern.

They ignored me. They ignored the wife-mother. I couldn't work out if they stepped around us or through us.

In order for the metabolism to keep going, for the grubs there in place of it to continue, physiological shocks are needed, almost exclusively in the head area: erasures of meaning, loss of worldly solidity, estrangement from humans. I was experiencing these shocks too frequently to exist as I should in the hallway. I'd clear the jitters only to contract them again. There was only a dull, pulseless, scoured-out calm, or the fear of that state (the cold, reflexive stare of that state turned ill and twitchy), itself a condition of the predictable monotony from the outside, but also of a terror from the inside, for which the only possible appeasement was to somehow return to the offending object.

I'd forgotten how it was to be nervous of existing. How the presence reclaimed was only the reconstitution of the former absence: electric shocks administered to a corpse.

I glanced behind me at the son to the right and his mother. I saw various parts of them together in the same place, on their hallway floor homogenizing. Their eyes and heads and limbs and hands all there intertwined in a hideous pulp of human tissues. There was none of the naturalness of merging, even with glass shards. They made the sound of someone straining to defecate. Neither was there any of the stillness required of the sanctum. In place of our translucent slime (as it was before the blood happened) was a disgusting secretion of two bodies dying.

It was as if my children didn't see them, as if the light no longer removed the walls for them to look that far. The wife-mother seemed not to exist for them either. They still divided their time between the door and the farthest point.

I assumed the posture of a human with a posture to assume, but nothing would convince them of my continued presence there.

The heads of my children radiated a darkness that the increasing brightness of the light was unable to remove. This darkness followed their heads, the assumed areas of their heads, in and out of the hallway. They were back breathing through their mouths and so they breathed it in and out when they breathed. It was a kind of pustulating smog. I'd seen it before on my screen around the heads of certain people who looked to be longing for something. More and more of them, faces asphyxiating in it, oblivious.

The universe is a mess. I find it hard to focus my eyes on a speck on the edge of my End key. The detail of the universe is a mess. I watch my screen for signs of life.

I heard what sounded like my children digging through the floor. I heard floorboards squeal. Somewhere far off I wanted to want to move.

Second-order desire is a conversation there are not enough of me to resume.

The light got so bright I could see nothing but an imagined view of grubs quailing in a ball beneath the faint gossamer of my skull. It was a crescendo that wouldn't end. The increases in brightness got so they were imperceptible, happening without being seen, but happening because they had to be, because there was only further and further, more and more, increase after increase, on and on until only darkness could approximate its unswerving acceleration.

I sat in the enforced blackness of the new light looking out.

The screen was gone. The wife-mother moving as if gone. The hallway gone. The reliquiae of what world there'd been: gone.

The grubs drank its blackness like it was my blood. I felt them swelling up on it. I felt my skin made of them feeling it. I felt them multiplying in the intensity of a light made through its excess to appear an exclusion of light.

I gorged on their gorging without me.

The black air obliterated their formation of my lungs. New organs were made for the new light.

My children had the purpose of animals that could see in the dark.

The universe took on the gruesomeness of an experiment.

My screen came back on. A dim glowing blur of the flat's outside.

The crowd in the street collapsed, as did the spectators on the landing and on the stairs: every one of them dead. They were replaced in minutes. Fresh bodies clustered in the road and filing through the building. I watched the replacements die. I watched the replacements of the replacements die.

In my Inbox was a notification of a post on the impracticalities of digging through floors to exit a sanctum. Excavating a hole in the floorboards and the ceiling plaster the other side was, it claimed, a simple procedure, but the possibility of transit through that hole was complicated by the air, which seemed to have solidified into something like metal on the underside.

I ate from my wife in darkness. I swallowed pieces of the broken mirror by mistake. One wedged in the throated area, where I'd choked on things before. I remembered then how my throat would sometimes choke on its own—on itself.

For a few seconds it seemed like my screen was floating there in front of my face. I imagined using my thoughts to control the cursor. Windows popped up and dropped away. Feeds updated. Notifications arrived. Communications. The footage was streaming there of more people dying. And there was something inconclusive about it, like it had happened at an earlier phase.

My thinking about choking was not enough to realize it. I felt the piece of mirror go down, the grubs pulling at it, surrounding it and easing its passage like some living lubricant. My consciousness of the organizational mechanics of my lower brain was suddenly more intimate than any relation I had to anything else. The grubs were talking back to me in a way the world couldn't or was refusing to. It struck me then that my children's grubs had probably died by now.

My children's bodies were not young anymore, or if they were they were not the pliable disease-free organisms their friends were. Their bodies had an indeterminate age, the age of things augmented beyond the point where temporality remains a relevant factor. My children's bodies were stretched materials. They swelled and sloughed and jutted and dripped in non-standardized ways. When they'd learned to walk this second time, they'd learned like dogs with missing limbs learn: compensating for the modification with accentuations of posture and balance that added something broadly supernatural to the medley of their adopted deformities.

My legs, crossed for days, went into spasm. I'd been staring into my screen, at windows popping up two a second, and had forgotten in the trance to move onto her back to merge.

Her smell had changed since the mirrors. It had changed since the increase in outside attention too, but more so since ingesting the glass. The smell was altered, but still not anything I could provide similes for. The smell up close made my grubs rage. New wars came on TV. New people were murdered by the same people. Viruses drank the plasma of a village, then a town, then a city. Weather licked the earth. Power stations fell through the ground. Entire countries puking up their organs into filthy toilets could not approximate her smell.

Since the deviation I'd posted more content than I'd read. The disclaimer drawing more activity, not less. Other contributors looked to be discovering uniquenesses of their own. One woman claimed her son had disappeared into the body of her father. She received the same treatment as me. Her testimonies could not be vouched for. There was always a residue. This disappearance gave the site a bad name. The content could only be so anomalous or there'd be no reliable inferences, no ease of reference, no credible claim to any sort of overview. The phases kept multiplying, crawling over each other like leaf-cutter ants across a pond that turned into a river, then a lake, then a sea.

The noise from the street got louder.

The air got cooler. More movement in it.

The crowd in the street was looking up in the direction of the webcam, which was what happened as standard, only it was every head at once; and I saw its attention shift suddenly just slightly to the right, to the other window, the window in the main room.

The crowd fitted with excitement. Whatever it was seeing was everything it had waited for. Everyone had at least one phone pointed at the main room window. It screamed in all its voices using the same few words. I didn't catch them. They sounded slurred, like the words my children spoke. The view flickered and sludged at the edges like degraded film stock.

Since the alteration in light I wasn't able to see through my eyelids, and sometimes the effort of keeping them open was more than I could make. But I saw long enough to know what I was seeing.

I saw long enough to see the crowd's outer layers covered in the remains of my daughter, to see their faces obscured by her, their coats and trousers and skirts peppered with parts of gradually diminishing size the farther away my eyes travelled from the point of impact. It wasn't from recognizing her in this newly abstracted form that I knew it was my daughter and not my son at the centre of this explosive defenestration, but because I could still hear my son in the main room, in front of the TV, screaming like foxes scream in the middle of the night.

I managed to see my daughter's failed escape from fifty or more different angles. It had become hard to tell, her morphing physicality conundrum-like in the perpetual indecision of its arrangement, but there was something resembling joy about her as she positioned herself at the open window. The way she exploded, even, was not without this joy, this inhuman joy, this joy that had left humanness behind it.

I thought of it as a failed escape, but I'm not always convinced of the veracity of that description.

It took them weeks to locate her remains. Parts of her were found in people's mouths two streets away, on the walls of the living rooms and bedrooms opposite, in the third ventricles of the brains of those fatally injured by her landing, in the stomachs of birds, in brickwork and doors and guttering, between the glazing in certain windows, in the fetus of an expectant mother who'd died quite coincidentally at the exact same moment my daughter hit the ground from congenital heart failure.

The pieces that were found could not be removed. There were those forced to wear my daughter's exploded organs as their faces until they died. I followed these people—subscribing to their blogs, adding them on social media—as a way of keeping in touch with the life my daughter was living since her death. Others would carry tiny parts of her around with them in their lungs and livers and hearts and kidneys, but these proved difficult to track down, as they were less public about it, if they realized she was there inside them at all.

The grubs at the front of my brain simulation, just behind my temples, which had remained in much the same place as before, turned septic.

My son made noises for days that made it seem each time like he was about to die. Finally he turned up in the doorway to the main room. His makeshift clothes were gone. In human terms he looked weak. All I saw was a distinct physiological trending toward recovery. Most contributors who made comments doubted it, but the incremental changes around his waist and neck seemed to dispute their scepticism.

With increasing slowness he returned to the wife-mother. I could see the difference in hunger in his eyes when he looked at her.

My son did not walk through me on his way to resuming his spot beside his mother. He clambered down onto the floor and started eating from her right away. As he gorged the slime I showed him images of broken mirrors on the screen of my laptop. He consumed without intermission. The shards were smaller by then than they had been and they went down, it seemed, without his noticing.

When he finished eating we sat there at opposite sides of her looking into our screens watching videos of the daughter-sister dying. I watched them in conjunction with the feed from the people on which she now lived. I emailed all the links to all her new existences to my son. There was something resembling recognition in the empty email he sent back.

We merged in turn and did not feel any guilt at having longer there than we'd had for many of the earlier phases, which I now considered to be either middle-phases or late-middle-phases.

Our audience started to shrink. The crowd thinned. There were fewer bodies on the landing and the stairs. The man from the ground floor flat turned up more frequently. His skin was hanging off and he was drooling blood. I could see he was still talking incessantly. What I couldn't see was anyone responding to him. Regardless of the density of the queue, there was always an arm's length perimeter of unoccupied space around him. What he said as he passed the door began to sound more like a language I knew, but ultimately the semantic overlap was too fleeting to effect any sort of credible translation.

My language centres were made of glass and slime. The wife-mother's flatulence rang out to me like the purest, most balanced aphorism.

The glass fragments not already dispensed and extracted by our feeding collected at the surface like crystalline silt. Its reflective properties were, in this state, ineffectual enough for us to gradually scrape the layer from her back onto the floor.

We couldn't see my immediate neighbours since the light had changed, but we heard someone to the right crashing into the hallway wall hard enough to smash the plaster on the other side. I imagined it was the son's head. I imagined it bleeding profusely and the skull becoming increasingly fractured.

My son, by this time, had torn out the hair he'd glued back and replaced it in the pile. I don't know what he used to fix them back in place, but his teeth took longer to dislodge, and he managed only one or two a day. By the time they were all out and back in the pile he'd spewed so much blood there could only have been slime and grubs left inside him to fill the space.

A gradual tenseness in my fingers made it hard to type. I blamed an overall tenseness in the grubs throughout my body, thought of my fingers as part of this continuum. I blamed for the grubs' disquiet the mirror pieces that had been swilling around in me for phase upon phase, making the sanctum seem less justified in its open-endedness.

A post went up on the site and was quickly removed. I had enough time to read it: *Maybe the grubs are not our accomplices.*

I set about reconstituting my daughter from all the parts of her I could find, from all the links to all the people and objects that carried her around with them. I collated every image I could locate and arranged them over and over in different configurations to look like her. I named the site after her. I emailed my son to help me, but he didn't reply.

My son began watching videos of things exploding on YouTube, Vimeo, wherever. At intervals, he turned his screen to face me so that I could watch them too. As far as I could tell he hadn't yet seen all the hundreds of videos of his sister exploding.

News of my son's completed return to the wife-mother was greeted by the core community of The Unyielding with sceptical enthusiasm. And while for some the anomalousness of our unit implied an integral unreliability, for others ours had become the source materials to watch. There were as yet no other errant attendees, no other incidents of explosion.

What was left of the crowd was shielded from the pavement below our windows by a toughened sheet of clear Perspex. Some, patently nervous about the penetrative potential of diminutive fragments of bone, wore protective goggles, helmets and outer garments of considerable thickness. Others wore nothing but shorts and T-shirts and breached the defences at every available opportunity. They all waited for my son's return. They all wanted to be there when he dropped, when like his sister he disseminated his singularity into the air.

A new video of my daughter's descent was posted on The Unyielding by Georgia96. It had been slowed down to 5 and 10 frames per second. It showed her whispering to her brother. It showed her gesturing to the crowd with what looked like a wave. It showed her skin spilling from the edges of her clothes. It showed her looking happy all the way down. It showed her exploding before she hit the ground.

There'd been no sound from either neighbour for two days. I'd been listening for them, both earbuds out, at the expense of the slowed-down largo of my daughter falling, of her dividing over and over in every possible direction, of her scattered merging with the surrounding area and everything in it.

My son had taken to crying into the back of his mother's head when merging. The approximation of crying was not exact, but it looked more like crying than it looked like anything else. I never saw him cry at any other time. I saw only his face lit by explosions that weren't his sister.

I saw pregnant women on the street, the wrong side of the Perspex, offering their tumescent stomachs to the explosion they envisioned my son becoming.

A news report confirmed the death of our immediate

neighbours, but not before I'd already been made aware of it via a homemade sign, held at arm's length above the heads of the diminishing crowd, by someone of nondescript gender that read: *Your Neighbours Have DIED*. Still I remained to be convinced, for they had nothing more to go on, I imagined, than their extended silence. And then the footage became available, uploaded to The Unyielding by some anonymous user, of them rotted out in their narrow hallways.

The man from downstairs stopped arriving outside our door, and about that time I considered him dead too.

I watched the crowd shrink on the street outside. More people walked up and down it, as they'd done before, and fewer and fewer stood still or even paused. Eventually the Perspex was removed. The footage from our webcams fed us a world we had no taste for, the landing and the stairs likewise increasingly empty of people for which we were the draw. We went back to the slow muted panic of being forgotten, even by ourselves.

Still we could not move her. And it wasn't, I was sure, anything to do with our efforts having been compromised by the years in attendance to it, to the immovability, for she remained the wife-mother.

The slime started to change colour. It became increasingly dark, emitted less of what I'd thought of as its glow. We put it down to the onset of the Black Light. Other well-established users at The Unyielding reported similar findings.

An email arrived from my son. At the bottom, above which there was just space demarcated as whiteness, he'd written only three words: *What will happen?* I shut it down without replying.

Another email arrived, again from him: same question. Just the look of him opposite me, the sludge of his eyes directed pleadingly at the computer in my lap, testified to some newly acquired compulsion.

I opened it, scrolled down through the space, and at the bottom wrote: *She might explode.*

Seconds later he replied. He wrote: *She might decay.*

I wrote: *She might stay as she is.*

He wrote: *She might disappear.*

I wrote: *She might become spatially unstable.*

He wrote: *She might become a liquid.*

I wrote: *She might become a powder.*

He wrote: *She might wake up.*

I wrote: *She might not remember us.*

He wrote: *She might start growing and not stop.*

I wrote: *She might devour us when we merge.*

He wrote: *She might speak.*

I wrote: *She might harden like a rock.*

He wrote: *She might become invisible.*

I wrote: *She might stay as she is.*

My use of repetition resulted in him shifting the focus onto us, and we hypothesized that we might *stay as we are, die, become like her, explode, expand, contract, leave, be taken, permanently merge, go back to how we were, get slowly eaten by cats or by insects, go mad, become air...* And ultimately: *How many more years will we wait?*

And beyond us we asked: *Will the sister-daughter regroup? Will this happen to everyone? Will the crowd come back? Will the world end around us? Will we be the last ones left? Will our devices stop working? Will the site go down?*

Of all these possibilities, none seemed right. We ran out of things to write without feeling we'd exhausted what might happen. I suspected, but didn't say, that what would happen would somehow not happen, not to us, not to her, and that its not happening would be the thing.

The grubs inside us were on the move: an intensely sensate peristalsis from the head down. I could see my son's skin bulging and sucking in corrugations repulsively fluid. His eyes were fixed on me. The wife-mother did not move.

The light deteriorated further till only the coloured light from our screens was visible. She and my son were indiscriminate blacknesses in the narrow hallway I imagined narrow, imagined a hallway, imagined myself in.

The movement I felt within my own body I imagined in my son.

My awareness seemed excessive and progressively unwanted. I crawled in the dark to merge, sometimes finding my son already there. Not wanting to return to my spot, I'd merge alongside him, slowly edging him off onto the floor.

I watched a video of a young girl whose puppy kept dying and coming back to life. It would die in the evening and be buried, only to return the next day. It turned out that the father had managed to acquire a litter of six almost indistinguishable dogs. He had killed the dogs each day and replaced them while she slept. He'd wanted his daughter to believe in something. He'd wanted her to have something the world could not take. He let the last one live. When eventually it died he hid the body and told her it had gone someplace else, to become a puppy again.

Watching the growing normalcy of her dog's resurrection take possession of her face concentrated my attention in a way I failed to understand.

I watched a puppy get eaten alive by someone's pet snake: same thing.

What will happen will be some continuation of our being alive. Obvious: yes. But it will come as a surprise. As if surely this was meant for someone else. Or rather for something better able to live it, some more complete version of this nothing.

The woman who wears part of my daughter's stomach across the left side of her face got married. I clicked through the wedding pictures. I saw nothing remarkable. When the vows were complete, the new husband kissed the side of her face where my daughter wasn't.

We became accustomed to the deteriorated light. It happened slowly, but my son, the wife-mother, and the narrow hallway eventually rematerialized unchanged from the unoccupied blankness. And then the light went bad again. And our eyes would once again familiarize themselves with its worsened state. And the things around us returned. And they went.

Once every few months a new user would join the site, but only about half of them turned out to be genuine. Our numbers stayed stable this way; for while nobody had yet reached a late-late phase, there had been more explosions, and implosions too, though only ever the attendees.

I watched a video of a thirty-three-year-old mother of twins collapse to the size of a duck egg, that due to its increased density was there on the screen for perhaps less than a second before it fell through the floor. This sudden concentration of grubs, which by this stage must have colonized the attendee's entire body (skin, bone, hair, the lot), could not be accounted for. It was as much a source of collective consternation as were the immovables themselves.

I was by this time less composed of thoughts than I was unmanifested twitches. What premises I considered and what conclusions I came to seemed to exist as the germs of something that was to follow them but never did.

One of these umanifested twitches would be the dimming memory of our existence before this, of what it had been to live as if the vague article of living itself was to become an accretion of who we were.

My son's eyes turned black and swelled to the size of apples. This had not been on our list of what might happen. But then nothing unwanted came of it, so its occurrence and its omission was either way of no lasting significance.

When I emailed him a picture of his face, he replied: *Yours too*, and sent me a picture of my own face, its eyes equally black and swollen to even greater proportions.

We figured the alteration to our eyes was nothing more

than a natural response to the deteriorated light. And that we were able to adapt so quickly made us temporarily more impressive to ourselves. When I wrote up my post for The Unyielding I closed it with an ellipsis, because there was more, of which this was only one small symptom.

Everything that had happened, to the wife-mother and to us, was a sequence of adaptive processes reacting to some larger, more pervasive and fundamental, set of conditions that up until then we and the world had colluded in hiding, of which our eyes, so recently blackened and inflated, were only an insignificant part.

The immovables were not only the earliest but also the most complete divergence. The attendees, all of us, were just trying to catch up. Our methods gave rise to mutations—our conscious emulations, our seduction—rendering us perpetually transitional, penumbral and precarious.

I did not want to post what the ellipsis contained until I could provide some detail, some scant adumbration, to what it was we had been responding to, what it was about the world and us in it that had brought about this errantly physiological abreaction. And, of course, once I'd happened on it, I could no longer stomach the prospect of putting it there, of disseminating it at all—even to my son, or myself for more than the most suffered of instants.

Once I knew, it was hard to see my wife as anything but the perfect human response to what was known. For all the apparent impotence and collapse, every immovable was in fact an impeccably realized and spontaneous solution, in comparison to which the attendee's emulations were an embarrassment.

The change in our eyes was, then, of metaphorical significance, allowing us to see in the dark when there was no point left in seeing in the dark.

And I was heading backwards: twitched awake somewhere inside myself when there was nothing left to excuse any such states of wakefulness.

We were the recalcitrants, the tragi-comic, flawed accompaniment to someone else's sublime, nonpareil epiphany.

I'd read about how the headaches would come, at some late phase of that interminably extended middle phase, or rather some single ache up there among the head, that did not pause for breath, acting like some veil of inflammation stifling what was left of the world or my thinking it. Because of what the headache denied me access to, I couldn't help but think of it as benign, as a survival mechanism initiated by my recent disclosure; which also meant those others that had already reported this affliction knew what I knew, and like me could not bring themselves to document it.

The headache became my head. There was no head there other than the ache it had.

I could not move to merge, and so my son stayed on top of her that much longer, these periods extending until he appeared to be sinking down inside of her, further or so it looked than should have been possible, given that the floor beneath would not permit the seepage of bodies.

I'm unsure as to the exact duration, but the solid mass of the ache that had swallowed my head began to crack, and in those cracks a muzziness started to form. There was something to it of the dream sequences found in films, a cloudy distortion to the edges of the frame. By the time my head returned I was uncertain how to occupy it.

I started paying too much attention to the details of what went on around me. I was after the sense of clarity the ache had taken. But the details, rather than alleviating the muzziness, only served to legitimate it.

Regardless of the hour of the day it always felt like I'd just woken up—without having properly woken up. It was my own head preventing me from waking up. My perpetually muzzy state some kind of replacement precaution, in place of the ache.

The grubs felt evenly distributed and sluggish in their movements.

Merging became less the compulsion it had been and more the habit it might have looked like to someone that might observe me. I did it because merging was what I'd done before. I did it because my son was waiting for me to do it. I merged like one would eat to stay alive.

I took on the slime from her back in the same way, the same labored justifications taking the place of what before had been instinctive.

I wanted the lucidity to return, but knew as well what would likely come with it, for while its content remained intact within me, so that I could think it in short bursts, it no longer permeated everything I saw—the glare of it the very light of consciousness itself. I had instead some dream of the dream of the world: I was buffered.

If my sight was holding something back, so too were my ears. The world came through muffled, droning. Pressure would build in them like I was experiencing extreme altitude. And the pressure did not abate. And I never heard what I wasn't supposed to hear. And though I never stood up I could tell my balance was off.

I knew that if the muzziness ever cleared I'd join the wife-mother—in that precise instant. I would become the first attendee to join the ranks of the immovables, and my son would be left with two bodies demanding that he merge with them. Ostensibly my son would be alone. And nobody at the forum would believe him. The tale of his anomalous father having breached the sanctum sanctorum of the still would incite members to acts of wordy disapprobation and threats of complete ostracism.

I was the remainder of what I'd discovered minus the feeling of it.

I was thinking too much to compensate for what I wasn't thinking, constantly checking what I remembered from some video, some image, some piece of text. I was looking at the narrow hallway like it was somehow imperative I keep track of it. And yet despite this vigilance my attention was impaired: it wandered places without me. I was forever coming to in the middle of my own thoughts.

Regardless of the time of day it would feel like I'd just woken up. Because I was never waking up. Because I knew what waking up had become. Because, more importantly, my body knew it wasn't made for it.

I watched my son watch videos of videos being watched by someone else. I watched his eyes dismantling all the many receding layers of recreational surveillance, and via his cam-feed watched what he watched.

I'd perfected the normality of our existence. My son had no access to the exertions I hid. My normality was exacting. If he noticed anything it was the sheen of just how normal I'd become. But he wouldn't have noticed that: it was only something that I could feel.

While there seemed to be more emotional content than I'd been used to, it was instead its absence that was being felt.

The problem was I'd reimagined how I'd been before, so there was no returning to it. And I even distrusted the sense of complacent at-home-ness that had made me susceptible to this epistemological rupture in the first place. As a result, any coming back to myself involved slipping back into a felt illusion, and it took longer every time and fitted less and less well.

That I could continue living so unchanged was a profanity.

How did what I'd come to realize not destroy more of what it had promised was already destroyed?

How could the lie ingratiate itself again without my even believing it?

Why was I still there when what had happened happened as if to prepare me for someplace else, or rather nothing else, but not this, not a continuation of the same?

I came to resent the wife-mother her deathless death.

I envied my son's easy nonhumanness.

More than anything I wanted the nothing I was promised.

I began watching videos of human suffering. I watched documentaries about men and women eaten alive by cancers and by madness. I watched the world's atrocities unfold: the Holocaust, the world wars, genocides perpetrated by the Ottoman Empire, the British Empire, the Khmer Rouge, the Tutsi... I watched humans suffer on this engorged scale in Zimbabwe, in North Korea, in Rwanda, in Srebrenica, in Bosnia and Herzegovina, in Croatia, in Liberia, in Bangladesh, in Sudan, in Guatemala, in the Soviet Union, in Cambodia, in Syria, in Iraq, in Turkey, in America, in Australia, in Tibet, in Indonesia... I saw humans eat themselves to death, drink themselves to death, starve themselves to death. I watched suicides, murders and state-sanctioned executions. I watched the bereaved and the abused being born all over again behind the eyes like mutilated cattle.

I watched humans and bits of humans bulldozed into piles...

I saw naked bodies leached of joy.

I saw need as needful and needless.

I saw humans under glass.

I saw how those that continued did so interstitially, how God was just one of many interstices (or lacunas).

I saw humans trying to transcend their humanness, and they tried not in an effort to become less human, but less real.

Nowhere in what I'd watched did any part of me appear that couldn't be attributed to some empathetic residue pooling in craters like tar.

If humans were uncomfortable it was only in virtue of not being dead.

If I was uncomfortable it was the false memory of having once been alive.

This new uncertainty was all I had, and nothing is had that cannot be more accurately described as a disease.

Genuine uncertainty is the truth of what is often called freedom, and it's a freedom that no one has or could have—a freedom that itself possesses.

My son's face would turn gloopy on his mother. I read that when it slides off into her another truer one will form. All the redundant features will have gone. They will coagulate somewhere else, somewhere hidden—as grubs jostling for space.

I knew that the inertia I needed was not one so readily confused with waiting: it was some atemporality of what had already arrived.

The absence still felt fugitive; I was restless somehow in the calm of being nothing.

I imagined the wife-mother dreaming our adherence. And that I was being dreamt had to it a consoling accuracy. But I couldn't believe it. I did my best to believe what I saw—the wife-mother, my son, the narrow hallway, the images on my screen—but what I saw did not need or warrant belief. I felt indentured to it and I was.

The users at The Unyielding were trapped there. They'd arrived in search of a home. A companionship of soiled sheets. All their many sequestered uglinesses composing an awful kind of beauty.

The beings I see on my screen are for the most part so

charmingly human I'm convinced that I can no longer be one of them. My disgust has gone, and with it any claim to kinship.

Because there's more to come I'll keep going. But only because of that; the content is irrelevant now.

It is 21:12 on a Saturday and this means nothing.

My name is some word that no longer arrives, and my forgetting it has become my name.

ABOUT THE AUTHOR

Gary J. Shipley is a writer and philosopher based in the UK. He has published work in various philosophy journals and literary journals. He's the founding and managing editor of Schism Press. Most recently, he is the author of *You With Your Memory Are Dead* (Civil Coping Mechanisms, 2016). You can find him online at Thek Prosthetics *www.garyjshipley. blogspot.com.*